John Dryden, Giovanni Boccaccio, Geoffrey Chaucer

Dryden's Fables

Tales in Verse Retold from Chaucer and Boccaccio

John Dryden, Giovanni Boccaccio, Geoffrey Chaucer

Dryden's Fables
Tales in Verse Retold from Chaucer and Boccaccio

ISBN/EAN: 9783744774529

Printed in Europe, USA, Canada, Australia, Japan

Cover: Foto ©Andreas Hilbeck / pixelio.de

More available books at **www.hansebooks.com**

COMPANION POETS.

VI

Routledge's Companion Poets.

PUBLISHED MONTHLY.

Uniform with this Volume.

Companion Poets

DRYDEN'S FABLES

TALES IN VERSE

RETOLD

FROM CHAUCER AND BOCCACCIO

BY

JOHN DRYDEN

EDITED WITH AN INTRODUCTION

BY

HENRY MORLEY, LL.D.

EMERITUS PROFESSOR OF ENGLISH LANGUAGE AND
LITERATURE AT UNIVERSITY COLLEGE
LONDON

LONDON
GEORGE ROUTLEDGE & SONS, LIMITED
BROADWAY, LUDGATE HILL
GLASGOW, MANCHESTER, AND NEW YORK
1891

Printed by BALLANTYNE, HANSON & CO.
Edinburgh and London

INTRODUCTION.

JOHN MILTON died at the age of sixty-six on Sunday the eighth of November 1674. John Dryden's age was then forty-three, and from that date till his own death, on the first of May in the year 1700, there was a period of a quarter of a century, during which he was, beyond comparison, the greatest living poet of this country. Some poets, like Cowley and Pope, achieve much in their youth. In others there is a slow growth of power. Keats won his place in literature and died before he reached the age of twenty-six; Shelley only lived to be thirty. If Dryden had died at thirty, his name would have been associated with some heroic verses on the death of Cromwell, and some welcoming of Charles II. to the throne, with one or two other occasional pieces in the fashion of the time when they were written. He did not come to his full strength until he reached the age of fifty. His best powers were spent in the momentous controversy which was practically settled by the Revolution of 1688, and he was on the losing side. Under William III. Dryden gave up his position as Poet Laureate by refusing to take the formal oath of allegiance to the new sovereign, and was left to suffer under change of times. Dryden's age was fifty-seven at the date of the English Revolution. He had used his unrivalled power on the losing side, and the mob of witlings who sat in the sun pelted him with party scorn and shallow criticism. He must have had some grim satisfaction in noting that the Whigs had no better poet than Thomas Shadwell to put in the place of laureate that John Dryden had left vacant. Shadwell died in 1692, and Nahum Tate was his successor; while the office of royal historiographer, which Dryden, and Shadwell after him, had held together with that of laureate, was given to Thomas Rymer. Rymer was in his own time thought to be a good critic because he laid down the law according to the passing fashion of his day, and was as positive of its perfection as a milliner is of to-day's shape of a bonnet that would have been a horror yesterday and will be out of date to-morrow.

Dryden had sons to care for, and a wife who needed cherishing; her reason failed after his death. He set to work upon a play—the tragedy of *Don Sebastian, King of Portugal*. It was produced in 1690, and showed growth of power in his work as dramatist. At the close of the preface to this play, after having said some words in defence of its comic episode, Dryden said, " I should beg pardon for these instances; but perhaps they may be of use to future poets in the conduct of their plays. At least, if I appear too positive, I am growing old, and thereby in the possession of some experience, which men in years will always assume for a right of talking. Certainly, if a man can ever have reason to set a value upon himself, 'tis when his ungenerous enemies are taking the advantage of the times upon him, to ruin him in his reputation. And, therefore, for once I will make bold to take the counsel of my old master, Virgil—

Tu ne cede malis, sed contra audentior ito."

In the same year (1690) Dryden followed Plautus and Molière with his successful comedy of *Amphitryon; or, The Two Sosias.* Then followed the opera of *King Arthur,* for which Purcell wrote the music. Ill health caused Dryden to leave to a younger dramatist the finishing of his play of *Cleomenes.*

But the story of an exiled prince looking for foreign
aid to the regaining of his kingdom was thought to
be tainted with political allusion, and the failure in
1692 of his *Love Triumphant* caused Dryden to
cease from writing for the stage. In the same year,
with aid from his two sons and from other poets,
Dryden published a complete translation of the
Satires of Juvenal and Persius. But when he had
ceased to look to the stage for income he relied
chiefly upon a translation of Virgil, with three
hundred and fifty subscribers of two guineas.
A hundred of them paid another three guineas
apiece towards the supply of plates, which were
old plates touched up. Jacob Tonson, the publisher, desired greatly that Dryden would add to
the popularity of his Virgil by dedicating it to
William III. The poet being obstinate in his re-
fusal, the publisher did what he could in the way of
loyal flattery by including among the touches to
the old plates of Ogilby's Virgil that were to be
used for decoration a general remodelling of the
nose of Æneas into conformity with the nose of
King William. Whereupon it was said—

" Old Jacob, by deep judgment swayed,
    To please the wise beholders,
Has placed old Nassau's hook-nosed head
    On poor old Æneas' shoulders.

" To make the parallel hold tack,
    Methinks there's little lacking ;
One took his father pick-a-back,
    And tother sent his packing."

In July 1697 Dryden's translation of Virgil was
published in a handsome folio, and bore noble
witness to the sustained power of the poet. As
Samuel Johnson said, " It satisfied his friends, and
for the most part silenced his enemies." The first
edition was sold in a few months, and the poet
earned by his long labour about thirteen hundred
pounds. Two months after the publication of
his Virgil, Dryden was invited to write the Ode

annually set to music and produced at a musical
meeting upon St. Cecilia's Day. The purpose of
the writer of such an ode was to give to the
composer of the music the utmost opportunity of
showing the resources of his art. Dryden accepted
the commission, and produced the famous Ode for
St. Cecilia's day, called "Alexander's Feast," in
further evidence of a maturity of power that showed
no taint of decay. The opportunities that poem
gave to the musician were not fully seized until the
Ode was set, in 1736, by Handel to the music now
always associated with it. "I am glad to hear
from all hands," wrote Dryden to Tonson, "that
my Ode is esteemed the best of all my poetry by
all the town. I thought so myself when I writ it ;
but, being old, I mistrusted my own judgment."

His age then was sixty-six. His health was failing. His son Charles was disabled by an accident
at Rome ; money was needed to bring the son home
and secure proper care for him. "If it please God
I must die of overstudy," Dryden said, "I cannot
spend my life better than in preserving his."

He thought of translating Homer, and did trans-
late the first book of the Iliad, but he had agreed
with Tonson for a book, of any kind he pleased,
which was to contain ten thousand verses, and for
which he was to be paid two hundred and fifty
guineas, which were to be made up to £300 on the
publication of a second edition. What pleased
him best was to transform into the style and
manner of his time some tales from Chaucer and
Boccaccio. That was the dying swan's song of
John Dryden, here given in a little book, very
unlike the folio in which it first appeared only a
few weeks before its author's death.

Dryden, then in his sixty-sixth year, had long
been suffering from gout and gravel. Erysipelas
had lately attacked one of his legs, but he worked on
with calm use of his unbroken power. In working
upon Chaucer, as he had worked on Virgil, and
would have worked on Homer had life lasted,

a great poet paid his homage to a greater poet ;
and in this case to an old master whom the
critical taste of his day, formed under French
influence, was unable to appreciate. His transfor-
mation of a language through which Nature herself
spoke, into the best form of the artificial seven-
teenth century style, *fin du siècle*, is full of interest.
Wit and vigour are not lost when it is Dryden
who reshapes old verses ; and there is something
pleasant to the fancy in the little masquerading
that brings Chaucer among us, stepping firmly
out in lace cravat and ruffles, and a natural hair
wig. Dressed by any other hand than Dryden's,
the wig would have been horse-hair and full-bot-
tomed, and the transformed friend a mere figure of
burlesque. But Dryden, a true poet, felt the power
of the elder and the better man, and while he used
the fashion of his day he brought it into touch with
Nature.

After the old man had spent wit and gallantry
upon the opening lines to the Duchess of Ormond,
who was alike worthy of honour for her goodness
and distinguished by her beauty, Dryden settled
down to his work with a quiet vigour that showed
no trace of disease, pain, and home trouble, or
of pale death with his hand upon the study door.
In the spring of 1699 Dryden delivered to his publisher seven thousand five hundred verses on account
of the ten thousand bargained for. In March 1700,
under the name of "Fables," the book was published ; and Dryden died on the next following May
Day ; fit day for Chaucer's welcome to a world
where all is harmony, and there can be no critics
except those who have been numbered with the just.

FABLES.

MADAM,—

The bard who first adorned our native tongue
Tuned to his British lyre this ancient song,
Which Homer might without a blush rehearse,
And leaves a doubtful palm in Virgil's verse :
He matched their beauties, where they most excel,
Of love sung better, and of arms as well.
Vouchsafe, illustrious Ormond, to behold
What power the charms of beauty had of old,
Nor wonder if such deeds of arms were done,
Inspired by two fair eyes that sparkled like your own.
If Chaucer by the best idea wrought,
And poets can divine each other's thought,
The fairest nymph before his eyes he set ;
And then the fairest was Plantagenet,
Who three contending princes made her prize,
And ruled the rival nations with her eyes ;
Who left immortal trophies of her fame,
And to the noblest order gave the name.
Like her, of equal kindred to the throne,
You keep her conquests, and extend your own :
As when the stars in their ethereal race,
At length have rolled around the liquid space,
At certain periods they resume their place,

From the same point of heaven their course advance,
And move in measures of their former dance ;
Thus after length of ages, she returns,
Restored in you, and the same place adorns :
Or you perform her office in the sphere,
Born of her blood, and make a new Platonic year.

   O true Plantagenet, O race divine
(For beauty still is fatal to the line),
Had Chaucer lived that angel-face to view,
Sure he had drawn his Emily from you ;
Or had you lived to judge the doubtful right,
Your noble Palamon had been the knight ;
And conquering Theseus from his side had sent
Your generous lord, to guide the Theban govern-
     ment.

   Time shall accomplish that ; and I shall see
A Palamon in him, in you an Emily.

   Already have the Fates your path prepared,
And sure presage your future sway declared :
When westward, like the sun, you took your way,
And from benighted Britain bore the day,
Blue Triton gave the signal from the shore,
The ready Nereids heard, and swam before
To smooth the seas ; a soft Etesian gale
But just inspired, and gently swelled the sail ;
Portunus took his turn, whose ample hand
Heaved up the lightened keel, and sunk the sand,
And steered the sacred vessel safe to land.
The land, if not restrained, had met your way,
Projected out a neck, and jutted to the sea.
Hibernia, prostrate at your feet, adored
In you the pledge of her expected lord,
Due to her isle ; a venerable name ;
His father and his grandsire known to fame ;
Awed by that house, accustomed to command,
The sturdy kerns in due subjection stand,
Nor hear the reins in any foreign hand.

   At your approach they crowded to the port,
And scarcely landed, you create a court ;
As Ormond's harbinger, to you they run,
For Venus is the promise of the sun.

The waste of civil wars, their towns destroyed,
Pales unhonoured, Ceres unemployed,
Were all forgot; and one triumphant day
Wiped all the tears of three campaigns away.
Blood, rapines, massacres, were cheaply bought,
So mighty recompense your beauty brought.
As when the dove returning bore the mark
Of earth restored to the long-labouring ark,
The relics of mankind, secure of rest,
Oped every window to receive the guest,
And the fair bearer of the message blessed :
So, when you came, with loud repeated cries,
The nation took an omen from your eyes,
And God advanced His rainbow in the skies,
To sign inviolable peace restored ;   [accord.
The saints with solemn shouts proclaimed the new

When at your second coming you appear
(For I foretell that millenary year),
The sharpened share shall vex the soil no more,
But earth unbidden shall produce her store ;
The land shall laugh, the circling ocean smile,
And Heaven's indulgence bless the holy isle.

Heaven from all ages has reserved for you
That happy clime, which venom never knew ;
Or if it had been there, your eyes alone
Have power to chase all poison but their own.

Now in this interval, which Fate has cast
Betwixt your future glories and your past,
This pause of power, 'tis Ireland's hour to mourn
While England celebrates your safe return,
By which you seem the seasons to command,
And bring our summers back to their forsaken land.

The vanquished isle our leisure must attend,
Till the fair blessing we vouchsafe to send ;
Nor can we spare you long, though often we may
The dove was twice employed abroad, before [lend.
The world was dried, and she returned no more.

Nor dare we trust so soft a messenger,
New from her sickness, to that northern air ;
Rest here a while your lustre to restore,
That they may see you, as you shone before,

For yet, the eclipse not wholly past, you wade
Through some remains and dimness of a shade.

A subject in his prince may claim a right,
Nor suffer him with strength impaired to fight;
Till force returns, his ardour we restrain,
And curb his warlike wish to cross the main.

Now past the danger, let the learned begin
The inquiry, where disease could enter in;
How those malignant atoms forced their way,
What in the faultless frame they found to make their
Where every element was weighed so well,   [prey,
That Heaven alone, who mixed the mass, could tell
Which of the four ingredients could rebel;
And where, imprisoned in so sweet a cage,
A soul might well be pleased to pass an age.

And yet the fine materials made it weak;
Porcelain by being pure is apt to break.
Even to your breast the sickness durst aspire,
And forced from that fair temple to retire,
Profanely set the holy place on fire.
In vain your lord, like young Vespasian, mourned,
When the fierce flames the sanctuary burned;
And I prepared to pay in verses rude
A most detested act of gratitude:
Even this had been your elegy, which now
Is offered for your health, the table of my vow.

Your angel sure our Morley's mind inspired,
To find the remedy your ill required,
As once the Macedon, by Jove's decree,
Was taught to dream an herb for Ptolemy:
Or Heaven, which had such over-cost bestowed
As scarce it could afford to flesh and blood,
So liked the frame, He would not work anew,
To save the charges of another you;
Or by His middle science did He steer,
And saw some great contingent good appear,
Well worth a miracle to keep you here,
And for that end preserved the precious mould,
Which all the future Ormonds was to hold;
And meditated, in His better mind,
An heir from you who may redeem the failing kind.

Blessed be the power which has at once restored
The hopes of lost succession to your lord,
Joy to the first and last of each degree,
Virtue to courts, and, what I longed to see,
To you the Graces, and the Muse to me.
   O daughter of the rose, whose cheeks unite
The differing titles of the red and white ;
Who heaven's alternate beauty well display,
The blush of morning and the milky way ;
Whose face is Paradise, but fenced from sin ;
For God in either eye has placed a cherubin. ·
   All is your lord's alone ; even absent, he
Employs the care of chaste Penelope.
For him you waste in tears your widowed hours,
For him your curious needle paints the flowers ;
Such works of old imperial dames were taught,
Such for Ascanius fair Elisa wrought.
   The soft recesses of your hours improve
The three fair pledges of your happy love :
All other parts of pious duty done,
You owe your Ormond nothing but a son,
To fill in future times his father's place,
And wear the garter of his mother's race.

Palamon and Arcite; or, The Knight's Tale.

FROM CHAUCER.

IN THREE BOOKS.

—◦◦◦—

BOOK I.

In days of old there lived, of mighty fame,
A valiant prince, and Theseus was his name;
A chief, who more in feats of arms excelled,
The rising nor the setting sun beheld.
Of Athens he was lord; much land he won,
And added foreign countries to his crown.
In Scythia with the warrior queen he strove,
Whom first by force he conquered, then by love;
He brought in triumph back the beauteous dame,
With whom her sister, fair Emilia, came.
With honour to his home let Theseus ride,
With Love to friend, and Fortune for his guide,
And his victorious army at his side.
I pass their warlike pomp, their proud array,
Their shouts, their songs, their welcome on the way;
But, were it not too long, I would recite
The feats of Amazons, the fatal fight
Betwixt the hardy queen and hero knight;
The town besieged, and how much blood it cost
The female army, and the Athenian host;
The spousals of Hippolyta the queen;
What tilts and tourneys at the feast were seen;
The storm at their return, the ladies' fear:
But these and other things I must forbear

The field is spacious I design to sow
With oxen far unfit to draw the plough :
The remnant of my tale is of a length
To tire your patience, and to waste my strength ;
And trivial accidents shall be forborne,
That others may have time to take their turn,
As was at first enjoined us by mine host,
That he, whose tale is best and pleases most,
Should win his supper at our common cost.
 And therefore where I left, I will pursue
This ancient story, whether false or true,
In hope it may be mended with a new.
The prince I mentioned, full of high renown,
In this array drew near the Athenian town ;
When, in his pomp and utmost of his pride
Marching, he chanced to cast his eye aside,
And saw a quire of mourning dames, who lay
By two and two across the common way :
At his approach they raised a rueful cry,
And beat their breasts, and held their hands on high,
Creeping and crying, till they seized at last
His courser's bridle and his feet embraced.
" Tell me," said Theseus, " what and whence you
    are
And why this funeral pageant you prepare ?
Is this the welcome of my worthy deeds,
To meet my triumph in ill-omened weeds ?
Or envy you my praise, and would destroy
With grief my pleasures, and pollute my joy ?
Or are you injured, and demand relief ?
Name your request, and I will ease your grief."
 The most in years of all the mourning train
Began ; but swounded first away for pain ;
Then scarce recovered spoke : " Nor envy we
Thy great renown, nor grudge thy victory ;
'Tis thine, O King, the afflicted to redress,
And fame has filled the world with thy success :
We wretched women sue for that alone,
Which of thy goodness is refused to none ;
Let fall some drops of pity on our grief,
If what we beg be just, and we deserve relief ;

For none of us who now thy grace implore,
But held the rank of sovereign queen before;
Till, thanks to giddy Chance, which never bears
That mortal bliss should last for length of years,
She cast us headlong from our high estate,
And here in hope of thy return we wait,
And long have waited in the temple nigh,
Built to the gracious goddess Clemency.
But reverence thou the power whose name it bears,
Relieve the oppressed, and wipe the widows' tears.
I, wretched I, have other fortunes seen,
The wife of Capaneus, and once a queen;
At Thebes he fell; cursed be the fatal day!
And all the rest thou seest in this array
To make their moan their lords in battle lost,
Before that town besieged by our confederate host.
But Creon, old and impious, who commands
The Theban city, and usurps the lands,
Denies the rites of funeral fires to those
Whose breathless bodies yet he calls his foes.
Unburned, unburied, on a heap they lie;
Such is their fate, and such his tyranny;
No friend has leave to bear away the dead,
But with their lifeless limbs his hounds are fed."
At this she shrieked aloud; the mournful train
Echoed her grief, and grovelling on the plain,
With groans, and hands upheld, to move his
      mind,
Besought his pity to their helpless kind.
   The Prince was touched, his tears began to flow,
And, as his tender heart would break in two,
He sighed; and could not but their fate deplore,
So wretched now, so fortunate before.
Then lightly from his lofty steed he flew,
And raising one by one the suppliant crew,
To comfort each, full solemnly he swore,
That by the faith which knights to knighthood bore,
And whate'er else to chivalry belongs,
He would not cease till he revenged their wrongs;
That Greece should see performed what he declared,
And cruel Creon find his just reward.

He said no more, but shunning all delay
Rode on, nor entered Athens on his way;
But left his sister and his queen behind,
And waved his royal banner in the wind,
Where in an argent field the god of war
Was drawn triumphant on his iron car;
Red was his sword and shield, and whole attire,
And all the godhead seemed to glow with fire;
Even the ground glittered where the standard flew
And the green grass was dyed to sanguine hue.
High on his pointed lance his pennon bore
His Cretan fight, the conquered Minotaur:
The soldiers shout around with generous rage,
And in that victory their own presage.
He praised their ardour, inly pleased to see
His host, the flower of Grecian chivalry.
All day he marched, and all the ensuing night,
And saw the city with returning light.
The process of the war I need not tell,
How Theseus conquered, and how Creon fell;
Or after, how by storm the walls were won,
Or how the victor sacked and burned the town;
How to the ladies he restored again
The bodies of their lords in battle slain;
And with what ancient rites they were interred;
All these to fitter time shall be deferred:
I spare the widows' tears, their woeful cries,
And howling at their husbands' obsequies;
How Theseus at these funerals did assist,
And with what gifts the mourning dames dismissed.
  Thus when the victor chief had Creon slain,
And conquered Thebes, he pitched upon the plain
His mighty camp, and when the day returned,
The country wasted and the hamlets burned,
And left the pillagers, to rapine bred,
Without control to strip and spoil the dead.
  There, in a heap of slain, among the rest,
Two youthful knights they found beneath a load
    oppressed
Of slaughtered foes, whom first to death they sent,
The trophies of their strength, a bloody monument.

Both fair, and both of royal blood they seemed,
Whom kinsmen to the crown the heralds deemed ;
That day in equal arms they fought for fame ;
Their swords, their shields, their surcoats were the
    same :
Close by each other laid they pressed the ground,
Their manly bosoms pierced with many a grisly
Nor well alive nor wholly dead they were, [wound ;
But some faint signs of feeble life appear ;
The wandering breath was on the wing to part,
Weak was the pulse, and hardly heaved the heart.
These two were sisters' sons ; and Arcite one,
Much famed in fields, with valiant Palamon.
From these their costly arms the spoilers rent,
And softly both conveyed to Theseus' tent :
Whom, known of Creon's line and cured with care,
He to his city sent as prisoners of the war ;
Hopeless of ransom, and condemned to lie
In durance, doomed a lingering death to die.

    This done, he marched away with warlike sound,
And to his Athens turned with laurels crowned,
Where happy long he lived, much loved, and more
But in a tower, and never to be loosed, [renowned.
The woeful captive kinsmen are enclosed.

    Thus year by year they pass, and day by day,
Till once ('twas on the morn of cheerful May)
The young Emilia, fairer to be seen
Than the fair lily on the flowery green,
More fresh than May herself in blossoms new
(For with the rosy colour strove her hue),
Waked, as her custom was, before the day,
To do the observance due to sprightly May ;
For sprightly May commands our youth to keep
The vigils of her night, and breaks their sluggard
    sleep ;
Each gentle breast with kindly warmth she moves ;
Inspires new flames, revives extinguished loves.
In this remembrance Emily ere day
Arose, and dressed herself in rich array ;
Fresh as the month, and as the morning fair,
Adown her shoulders fell her length of hair :

A riband did the braided tresses bind,
The rest was loose and wantoned in the wind :
Aurora had but newly chased the night,
And purpled o'er the sky with blushing light,
When to the garden-walk she took her way,
To sport and trip along in cool of day,
And offer maiden vows in honour of the May.
   At every turn she made a little stand,
And thrust among the thorns her lily hand
To draw the rose ; and every rose she drew,
She shook the stalk, and brushed away the
    dew ;
Then parti-coloured flowers of white and red
She wove, to make a garland for her head :
This done, she sung and carolled out so clear,
That men and angels might rejoice to hear ;
Even wondering Philomel forgot to sing,
And learned from her to welcome in the spring.
The tower, of which before was mention made,
Within whose keep the captive knights were laid,
Built of a large extent, and strong withal,
Was one partition of the palace wall ;
The garden was enclosed within the square,
Where young Emilia took the morning air.
   It happened Palamon, the prisoner knight,
Restless for woe, arose before the light,
And with his jailer's leave desired to breathe
An air more wholesome than the damps beneath.
This granted, to the tower he took his way,
Cheered with the promise of a glorious day ;
Then cast a languishing regard around,
And saw with hateful eyes the temples crowned
With golden spires, and all the hostile ground.
He sighed, and turned his eyes, because he knew
'Twas but a larger jail he had in view ;
Then looked below, and from the castle's height
Beheld a nearer and more pleasing sight ;
The garden, which before he had not seen,
In spring's new livery clad of white and green,
Fresh flowers in wide parterres, and shady walks
    between.

This viewed, but not enjoyed, with arms across
He stood, reflecting on his country's loss ;
Himself an object of the public scorn,
And often wished he never had been born.
At last (for so his destiny required),
With walking giddy, and with thinking tired,
He through a little window cast his sight,
Though thick of bars, that gave a scanty light ;
But even that glimmering served him to descry
The inevitable charms of Emily.

Scarce had he seen, but, seized with sudden smart,
Stung to the quick, he felt it at his heart ;
Struck blind with overpowering light he stood,
Then started back amazed, and cried aloud.

Young Arcite heard ; and up he ran with haste,
To help his friend, and in his arms embraced ;
And asked him why he looked so deadly wan,
And whence, and how, his change of cheer began?
Or who had done the offence ? " But if," said he,
" Your grief alone is hard captivity,
For love of Heaven with patience undergo
A cureless ill, since Fate will have it so :
So stood our horoscope in chains to lie,
And Saturn in the dungeon of the sky,
Or other baleful aspect, ruled our birth,
When all the friendly stars were under earth :
Whate'er betides, by Destiny 'tis done ;
And better bear like men than vainly seek to shun."
" Nor of my bonds," said Palamon again,
" Nor of unhappy planets I complain ;
But when my mortal anguish caused my cry,
The moment I was hurt through either eye ;
Pierced with a random shaft, I faint away,
And perish with insensible decay :
A glance of some new goddess gave the wound,
Whom, like Actæon, unaware I found.
Look how she walks along yon shady space ;
Not Juno moves with more majestic grace,
And all the Cyprian queen is in her face.
If thou art Venus (for thy charms confess
That face was formed in heaven), nor art thou less,

Disguised in habit, undisguised in shape,
O help us captives from our chains to scape!
But if our doom be past in bonds to lie
For life, and in a loathsome dungeon die,
Then be thy wrath appeased with our disgrace,
And show compassion to the Theban race,
Oppressed by tyrant power!"—While yet he spoke,
Arcite on Emily had fixed his look;
The fatal dart a ready passage found
And deep within his heart infixed the wound:
So that if Palamon were wounded sore,
Arcite was hurt as much as he or more:
Then from his inmost soul he sighed, and said,
"The beauty I behold has struck me dead:
Unknowingly she strikes, and kills by chance;
Poison is in her eyes, and death in every glance.
Oh, I must ask; nor ask alone, but move
Her mind to mercy, or must die for love."
　　Thus Arcite: and thus Palamon replies
(Eager his tone, and ardent were his eyes),
"Speak'st thou in earnest, or in jesting vein?"
"Jesting,' said Arcite, "suits but ill with pain."
"It suits far worse' (said Palamon again,
And bent his brows), "with men who honour weigh,
Their faith to break, their friendship to betray;
But worst with thee, of noble lineage born,
My kinsman, and in arms my brother sworn.
Have we not plighted each our holy oath,
That one should be the common good of both;
One soul should both inspire, and neither prove
His fellow's hindrance in pursuit of love?
To this before the gods we gave our hands,
And nothing but our death can break the bands.
This binds thee, then, to further my design,
As I am bound by vow to further thine:
Nor canst, nor darest thou, traitor, on the plain
Appeach my honour, or thy own maintain,
Since thou art of my council, and the friend
Whose faith I trust, and on whose care depend.
And wouldst thou court my lady's love, which I
Much rather than release, would choose to die?

B

But thou, false Arcite, never shalt obtain,
Thy bad pretence; I told thee first my pain:
For first my love began ere thine was born;
Thou as my council, and my brother sworn,
Art bound to assist my eldership of right,
Or justly to be deemed a perjured knight."
   Thus Palamon: but Arcite with disdain
In haughty language thus replied again:
"Forsworn thyself: the traitor's odious name
I first return, and then disprove thy claim.
If love be passion, and that passion nurst
With strong desires, I loved the lady first.
Canst thou pretend desire, whom zeal inflamed
To worship, and a power celestial named?
Thine was devotion to the blest above,
I saw the woman, and desired her love;
First owned my passion, and to thee commend
The important secret, as my chosen friend.
Suppose (which yet I grant not) thy desire
A moment elder than my rival fire;
Can chance of seeing first thy title prove?
And knowst thou not, no law is made for love?
Law is to things which to free choice relate;
Love is not in our choice, but in our fate;
Laws are not positive; love s power we see
Is nature's sanction, and her first decree.
Each day we break the bond of human laws
For love, and vindicate the common cause.
Laws for defence of civil rights are placed, [waste.
Love throws the fences down, and makes a general
Maids, widows, wives without distinction fall;
The sweeping deluge, love, comes on and covers all.
If then the laws of friendship I transgress,
I keep the greater, while I break the less;
And both are mad alike, since neither can possess.
Both hopeless to be ransomed, never more
To see the sun, but as he passes o'er.
Like Æsop's hounds contending for the bone,
Each pleaded right, and would be lord alone;
The fruitless fight continued all the day,
A cur came by and snatched the prize away.

As courtiers therefore justle for a grant,
And when they break their friendship, plead their
So thou, if Fortune will thy suit advance,   [want,
Love on, nor envy me my equal chance :
For I must love, and am resolved to try
My fate, or failing in the adventure die."
  Great was their strife, which hourly was renewed,
Till each with mortal hate his rival viewed :
Now friends no more, nor walking hand in hand ;
But when they met, they made a surly stand,
And glared like angry lions as they passed,
And wished that every look might be their last.
  It chanced at length Pirithous came to attend
This worthy Theseus, his familiar friend :
Their love in early infancy began,
And rose as childhood ripened into man,
Companions of the war ; and loved so well,
That when one died, as ancient stories tell,
His fellow to redeem him went to hell.
  But to pursue my tale : to welcome home
His warlike brother is Pirithous come :
Arcite of Thebes was known in arms long since,
And honoured by this young Thessalian prince.
Theseus, to gratify his friend and guest,
Who made our Arcite's freedom his request,
Restored to liberty the captive knight,
But on these hard conditions I recite :
That if hereafter Arcite should be found
Within the compass of Athenian ground,
By day or night, or on whate'er pretence,
His head should pay the forfeit of the offence.
To this Pirithous for his friend agreed,
And on his promise was the prisoner freed.
  Unpleased and pensive hence he takes his way,
At his own peril ; for his life must pay.
Who now but Arcite mourns his bitter fate,
Finds his dear purchase, and repents too late ?
" What have I gained," he said, " in prison pent,
If I but change my bonds for banishment ?
And banished from her sight, I suffer more
In freedom than I felt in bonds before ;

Forced from her presence and condemned to live,
Unwelcome freedom and unthanked reprieve :
Heaven is not but where Emily abides,
And where she's absent, all is hell besides.
Next to my day of birth, was that accurst
Which bound my friendship to Pirithous first :
Had I not known that prince, I still had been
In bondage, and had still Emilia seen :
For though I never can her grace deserve,
'Tis recompense enough to see and serve.
O Palamon, my kinsman and my friend,
How much more happy fates thy love attend !
Thine is the adventure, thine the victory,
Well has thy fortune turned the dice for thee :
Thou on that angel's face mayest feed thy eyes,
In prison, no ; but blissful paradise !
Thou daily seest that sun of beauty shine,
And lov'st at least in love's extremest line.
I mourn in absence, love's eternal night ;
And who can tell but since thou hast her sight,
And art a comely, young, and valiant knight,
Fortune (a various power) may cease to frown,
And by some ways unknown thy wishes crown ?
But I, the most forlorn of human kind,
Nor help can hope nor remedy can find ;
But doomed to drag my loathsome life in care,
For my reward, must end it in despair.
Fire, water, air, and earth, and force of fates
That governs all, and Heaven that all creates,
Nor art, nor nature's hand can ease my grief ;
Nothing but death, the wretch's last relief :
Then farewell youth, and all the joys that dwell
With youth and life, and life itself, farewell !
    But why, alas ! do mortal men in vain
Of Fortune, Fate, or Providence complain ?
God gives us what He knows our wants require,
And better things than those which we desire :
Some pray for riches ; riches they obtain ;
But, watched by robbers, for their wealth are slain ;
Some pray from prison to be freed ; and come,
When guilty of their vows, to fall at home ;

Murdered by those they trusted with their life,
A favoured servant or a bosom wife.
Such dear-bought blessings happen every day,
Because we know not for what things to pray.
Like drunken sots about the streets we roam :
Well knows the sot he has a certain home,
Yet knows not how to find the uncertain place,
And blunders on, and staggers every pace.
Thus all seek happiness ; but few can find,
For far the greater part of men are blind.
This is my case, who thought our utmost good
Was in one word of freedom understood :
The fatal blessing came : from prison free,
I starve abroad, and lose the sight of Emily."
    Thus Arcite : but if Arcite thus deplore
His sufferings, Palamon yet suffers more.
For when he knew his rival freed and gone,
He swells with wrath ; he makes outrageous moan ;
He frets, he fumes, he stares, he stamps the ground ;
The hollow tower with clamours rings around :
With briny tears he bathed his fettered feet,
And dropped all o'er with agony of sweat.
"Alas !" he cried, " I, wretch, in prison pine,
Too happy rival, while the fruit is thine :
Thou liv'st at large, thou draw'st thy native air,
Pleased with thy freedom, proud of my despair :
Thou may'st, since thou hast youth and courage
        joined,
A sweet behaviour and a solid mind,
Assemble ours, and all the Theban race,
To vindicate on Athens thy disgrace ;
And after (by some treaty made) possess
Fair Emily, the pledge of lasting peace.
So thine shall be the beauteous prize, while I
Must languish in despair, in prison die.
Thus all the advantage of the strife is thine,
Thy portion double joys, and double sorrows mine."
    The rage of jealousy then fired his soul,
And his face kindled like a burning coal :
Now cold despair, succeeding in her stead,
To livid paleness turns the glowing red.

His blood, scarce liquid, creeps within his veins,
Like water which the freezing wind constrains.
Then thus he said : " Eternal Deities,
Who rule the world with absolute decrees,
And write whatever time shall bring to pass
With pens of adamant on plates of brass ;
What is the race of human kind your care
Beyond what all his fellow-creatures are?
He with the rest is liable to pain,
And like the sheep, his brother-beast, is slain.
Cold, hunger, prisons, ills without a cure,
All these be must, and guiltless oft, endure ;
Or does your justice, power, or prescience fail,
When the good suffer and the bad prevail ?
What worse to wretched virtue could befall,
If Fate or giddy Fortune governed all ?
Nay, worse than other beasts is our estate :
Them, to pursue their pleasures, you create ;
We, bound by harder laws, must curb our will,
And your commands, not our desires, fulfil :
Then, when the creature is unjustly slain,
Yet, after death at least, he feels no pain ;
But man in life surcharged with woe before,
Not freed when dead, is doomed to suffer more.
A serpent shoots his sting at unaware ;
An ambushed thief forelays a traveller ;
The man lies murdered, while the thief and
    snake,
One gains the thicket, and one threads the brake.
This let divines decide ; but well I know,
Just or unjust, I have my share of woe :
Through Saturn seated in a luckless place,
And Juno's wrath that persecutes my race ;
Or Mars and Venus in a quartil move
My pangs of jealousy for Arcite's love."
    Let Palamon oppressed in bondage mourn,
While to his exiled rival we return.
By this the sun, declining from his height,
The day had shortened to prolong the night :
The lengthened night gave length of misery,
Both to the captive lover and the free :

For Palamon in endless prison mourns,
And Arcite forfeits life if he returns ;
The banished never hopes his love to see,
Nor hopes the captive lord his liberty.
'Tis hard to say who suffers greater pains ;
One sees his love, but cannot break his chains ;
One free, and all his motions uncontrolled,
Beholds whate'er he would but what he would be-
Judge as you please, for I will haste to tell   [hold.
What fortune to the banished knight befell.
When Arcite was to Thebes returned again,
The loss of her he loved renewed his pain ;
What could be worse than never more to see
His life, his soul, his charming Emily?
He raved with all the madness of despair,
He roared, he beat his breast, he tore his hair.
Dry sorrow in his stupid eyes appears,
For wanting nourishment, he wanted tears ;
His eyeballs in their hollow sockets sink,
Bereft of sleep ; he loathes his meat and drink ;
He withers at his heart, and looks as wan
As the pale spectre of a murdered man :
That pale turns yellow, and his face receives
The faded hue of sapless boxen leaves ;
In solitary groves he makes his moan,
Walks early out, and ever is alone ;
Nor, mixed in mirth, in youthful pleasure shares,
But sighs when songs and instruments he hears.
His spirits are so low, his voice is drowned,
He hears as from afar, or in a swound,
Like the deaf murmurs of a distant sound :
Uncombed his locks, and squalid his attire,
Unlike the trim of love and gay desire ;
But full of museful mopings, which presage
The loss of reason and conclude in rage.
      This when he had endured a year and more,
Now wholly changed from what he was before,
It happened once, that, slumbering as he lay,
He dreamt (his dream began at break of day)
That Hermes o'er his head in air appeared,
And with soft words his drooping spirits cheered ;

His hat adorned with wings disclosed the god,
And in his hand he bore the sleep-compelling rod ;
Such as he seemed, when, at his sire's command,
On Argus' head he laid the snaky wand.
" Arise," he said, " to conquering Athens go ;
There fate appoints an end of all thy woe."
The fright awakened Arcite with a start,
Against his bosom bounced his heaving heart ;
But soon he said, with scarce recovered breath,
" And thither will I go to meet my death,
Sure to be slain ; but death is my desire,
Since in Emilia's sight I shall expire."
By chance he spied a mirror while he spoke,
And gazing there beheld his altered look ;
Wondering, he saw his features and his hue
So much were changed, that scarce himself he knew.
A sudden thought then starting in his mind,
" Since I in Arcite cannot Arcite find,
The world may search in vain with all their eyes,
But never penetrate through this disguise.
" Thanks to the change which grief and sickness
      give,
In low estate I may securely live,
And see, unknown, my mistress day by day."
He said, and clothed himself in coarse array,
A labouring hind in show ; then forth he went,
And to the Athenian towers his journey bent :
One squire attended in the same disguise,
Made conscious of his master's enterprise.
Arrived at Athens, soon he came to court,
Unknown, unquestioned in that thick resort :
Proffering for hire his service at the gate,
To drudge, draw water, and to run or wait.
    So fair befell him, that for little gain
He served at first Emilia's chamberlain ;
And, watchful all advantages to spy,
Was still at hand, and in his master's eye ;
And as his bones were big, and sinews strong,
Refused no toil that could to slaves belong ;
But from deep wells with engines water drew,
And used his noble hands the wood to hew.

He passed a year at least attending thus
On Emily, and called Philostratus.
But never was there man of his degree
So much esteemed, so well beloved as he.
So gentle of condition was he known,
That through the court his courtesy was blown :
All think him worthy of a greater place,
And recommend him to the royal grace ;
That exercised within a higher sphere.
His virtues more conspicuous might appear.
Thus by the general voice was Arcite praised,
And by great Theseus to high favour raised ;
Among his menial servants first enrolled,
And largely entertained with sums of gold :
Besides what secretly from Thebes was sent,
Of his own income and his annual rent.
This well employed, he purchased friends and fame
But cautiously concealed from whence it came.
Thus for three years he lived with large increase
In arms of honour, and esteem in peace ;
To Theseus person he was ever near,
And Theseus for his virtues held him dear.

BOOK II.

WHILE Arcite lives in bliss, the story turns
Where hopeless Palamon in prison mourns.
For six long years immured, the captive knight
Had dragged his chains, and scarcely seen the light ;
Lost liberty and love at once he bore ;
His prison pained him much, his passion more :
Nor dares he hope his fetters to remove,
Nor ever wishes to be free from love.
    But when the sixth revolving year was run,
And May within the Twins received the sun,
Were it by Chance, or forceful Destiny,
Which forms in causes first whate'er shall be,
Assisted by a friend one moonless night,
This Palamon from prison took his flight ;

A pleasant beverage he prepared before
Of wine and honey mixed, with added store
Of opium ; to his keeper this he brought,
Who swallowed unaware the sleepy draught,
And snored secure till morn, his senses bound
In slumber, and in long oblivion drowned.
Short was the night, and careful Palamon
Sought the next covert ere the rising sun.
A thick-spread forest near the city lay,
To this with lengthened strides he took his way
(For far he could not fly, and feared the day).
Safe from pursuit, he meant to shun the light,
Till the brown shadows of the friendly night
To Thebes might favour his intended flight.
When to his country come, his next design
Was all the Theban race in arms to join,
And war on Theseus, till he lost his life,
Or won the beauteous Emily to wife.
Thus while his thoughts the lingering day beguile,
To gentle Arcite let us turn our style ;
Who little dreamt how nigh he was to care,
Till treacherous fortune caught him in the snare.
The morning-lark, the messenger of day,
Saluted in her song the morning grey ;
And soon the sun arose with beams so bright,
That all the horizon laughed to see the joyous sight ;
He with his tepid rays the rose renews,
And licks the dropping leaves, and dries the dews ;
When Arcite left his bed, resolved to pay
Observance to the month of merry May.
Forth on his fiery steed betimes he rode,
That scarcely prints the turf on which he trod :
At ease he seemed, and prancing o'er the plains,
Turned only to the grove his horse's reins,
The grove I named before, and, lighting there,
A woodbine garland sought, to crown his hair ;
Then turned his face against the rising day,
And raised his voice to welcome in the May :
    " For thee, sweet month, the groves green liveries
        wear,
If not the first, the fairest of the year :

For thee the Graces lead the dancing hours,
And nature's ready pencil paints the flowers:
When thy short reign is past, the feverish sun
The sultry tropic fears, and moves more slowly on.
So may thy tender blossoms fear no blight,
Nor goats with venomed teeth thy tendrils bite,
As thou shalt guide my wandering feet to find
The fragrant greens I seek, my brows to bind."
    His vows addressed, within the grove he strayed,
Till Fate or Fortune near the place conveyed
His steps where secret Palamon was laid.
Full little thought of him the gentle knight,
Who flying death had there concealed his flight,
In brakes and brambles hid, and shunning mortal
And less he knew him for his hated foe,   [sight;
But feared him as a man he did not know.
But as it has been said of ancient years,
That fields are full of eyes and woods have ears,
For this the wise are ever on their guard,
For unforeseen, they say, is unprepared.
Uncautious Arcite thought himself alone,
And less than all suspected Palamon,
Who, listening, heard him, while he searched the
And loudly sung his roundelay of love: [grove,
But on the sudden stopped, and silent stood
(As lovers often muse, and change their mood);
Now high as heaven, and then as low as hell,
Now up, now down, as buckets in a well:
For Venus, like her day, will change her cheer,
And seldom shall we see a Friday clear.
Thus Arcite, having sung, with altered hue
Sunk on the ground, and from his bosom drew
A desperate sigh, accusing Heaven and Fate,
And angry Juno's unrelenting hate:
"Cursed be the day when first I did appear;
Let it be blotted from the calendar,
Lest it pollute the month, and poison all the year,
Still will the jealous Queen pursue our race?
Cadmus is dead, the Theban city was:
Yet ceases not her hate; for all who come
From Cadmus are involved in Cadmus' doom.

I suffer for my blood : unjust decree,
That punishes another's crime on me.
In mean estate I serve my mortal foe,
The man who caused my country's overthrow.
This is not all ; for Juno, to my shame,
Has forced me to forsake my former name ;
Arcite I was, Philostratus I am.
That side of heaven is all my enemy ;
Mars ruined Thebes ; his mother ruined me.
Of all the royal race remains but one
Besides myself, the unhappy Palamon,
Whom Theseus holds in bonds and will not free ;
Without a crime, except his kin to me.
Yet these and all the rest I could endure ;
But love's a malady without a cure :
Fierce Love has pierced me with his fiery dart,
He fries within, and hisses at my heart.
Your eyes, fair Emily, my fate pursue ;
I suffer for the rest, I die for you.
Of such a goddess no time leaves record,
Who burned the temple where she was adored :
And let it burn, I never will complain,
Pleased with my sufferings, if you knew my pain."
    At this a sickly qualm his heart assailed,
His ears ring inward, and his senses failed.
No word missed Palamon of all he spoke ;
But soon to deadly pale he changed his look :
He trembled every limb, and felt a smart,
As if cold steel had glided through his heart ;
Nor longer stayed, but starting from his place,
Discovered stood, and showed his hostile face :
    " False traitor, Arcite, traitor to thy blood,
Bound by thy sacred oath to seek my good,
Now art thou found forsworn for Emily,
And dar'st attempt her love, for whom I die.
So hast thou cheated Theseus with a wile,
Against thy vow returning to beguile
Under a borrowed name : as false to me,
So false thou art to him who set thee free.
But rest assured, that either thou shalt die,
Or else renounce thy claim in Emily ;

For though unarmed I am, and, freed by chance,
Am here without my sword or pointed lance,
Hope not, base man, unquestioned hence to go,
For I am Palamon, thy mortal foe."
  Arcite, who heard his tale and knew the man,
His sword unsheathed, and fiercely thus began :
" Now, by the gods who govern heaven above,
Wert thou not weak with hunger, mad with love,
That word had been thy last ; or in this grove
This hand should force thee to renounce thy love ;
The surety which I gave thee I defy :
Fool, not to know that love endures no tie,
And Jove but laughs at lovers' perjury.
Know, I will serve the fair in thy despite ;
But since thou art my kinsman and a knight,
Here have my faith, to-morrow in this grove
Our arms shall plead the titles of our love :
And Heaven so help my right, as I alone
Will come, and keep the cause and quarrel both
    unknown,
With arms of proof both for myself and thee ;
Choose thou the best, and leave the worst to me.
And, that at better ease thou mayest abide,
Bedding and clothes I will this night provide,
And needful sustenance, that thou may'st be
A conquest better won, and worthy me."
His promise Palamon accepts ; but prayed,
To keep it better than the first he made.
Thus fair they parted till the morrow's dawn ;
For each had laid his plighted faith to pawn.
Oh Love ! thou sternly dost thy power maintain,
And wilt not bear a rival in thy reign !
Tyrants and thou all fellowship disdain.
This was in Arcite proved and Palamon :
Both in despair, yet each would love alone.
Arcite returned, and, as in honour tied,
His foe with bedding and with food supplied ;
Then, ere the day, two suits of armour sought,
Which borne before him on his steed he brought :
Both were of shining steel, and wrought so pure
As might the strokes of two such arms endure.

Now, at the time, and in the appointed place,
The challenger and challenged, face to face,
Approach ; each other from afar they knew,
And from afar their hatred changed their hue.
So stands the Thracian herdsman with his spear,
Full in the gap, and hopes the hunted bear,
And hears him rustling in the wood, and sees
His course at distance by the bending trees :
And thinks, Here comes my mortal enemy,
And either he must fall in fight, or I :
This while he thinks, he lifts aloft his dart ;
A generous chillness seizes every part,
The veins pour back the blood, and fortify the heart.
    Thus pale they meet ; their eyes with fury burn ;
None greets, for none the greeting will return ;
But in dumb surliness each armed with care
His foe professed, as brother of the war ;
Then both, no moment lost, at once advance
Against each other, armed with sword and lance :
They lash, they foin, they pass, they strive to bore
    Their corslets, and the thinnest parts explore.
Thus two long hours in equal arms they stood,
And wounded wound, till both were bathed in blood
And not a foot of ground had either got,
As if the world depended on the spot.
Fell Arcite like an angry tiger fared,
And like a lion Palamon appeared :
Or, as two boars whom love to battle draws,
With rising bristles and with frothy jaws,
Their adverse breasts with tusks oblique they wound,
With grunts and groans the forest rings around.
So fought the knights, and fighting must abide,
Till Fate an umpire sends their difference to decide.
The power that ministers to God's decrees,
And executes on earth what Heaven foresees,
Called Providence, or Chance. or Fatal sway,
Comes with resistless force, and finds or makes her way.
Nor kings, nor nations, nor united power
One moment can retard the appointed hour ;

And some one day some wondrous chance appears
Which happened not in centuries of years :
For sure, whate'er we mortals hate or love
Or hope or fear depends on powers above :
They move our appetites to good or ill,
And by foresight necessitate the will.
In Theseus this appears, whose youthful joy
Was beasts of chase in forests to destroy ;
This gentle knight, inspired by jolly May,
Forsook his easy couch at early day,
And to the wood and wilds pursued his way.
Beside him rode Hippolyta the queen,
And Emily attired in lively green,
With horns and hounds and all the tuneful cry,
To hunt a royal hart within the covert nigh :
And, as he followed Mars before, so now
He serves the goddess of the silver bow.
The way that Theseus took was to the wood,
Where the two knights in cruel battle stood :
The laund on which they fought, the appointed place
In which the uncoupled hounds began the chase.
Thither forthright he rode to rouse the prey,
That shaded by the fern in harbour lay ;
And thence dislodged, was wont to leave the wood
For open fields, and cross the crystal flood.
Approached, and looking underneath the sun,
He saw proud Arcite and fierce Palamon,
In mortal battle doubling blow on blow ;
Like lightning flamed their faulchions to and fro,
And shot a dreadful gleam ; so strong they strook,
There seemed less force required to fell an oak.
He gazed with wonder on their equal might,
Looked eager on, but knew not either knight.
Resolved to learn, he spurred his fiery steed
With goring rowels to provoke his speed.
The minute ended that began the race,
So soon he was betwixt them on the place ;
And with his sword unsheathed, on pain of life
Commands both combatants to cease their strife ;
Then with imperious tone pursues his threat :
" What are you ? why in arms together met ?

How dares your pride presume against my laws,
As in a listed field to fight your cause,
Unasked the royal grant ; no marshal by,
As knightly rites require, nor judge to try?"
Then Palamon, with scarce recovered breath,
Thus hasty spoke : " We both deserve the death,
And both would die ; for look the world around,
A pair so wretched is not to be found.
Our life's a load ; encumbered with the charge,
We long to set the imprisoned soul at large.
Now, as thou art a sovereign judge, decree
The rightful doom of death to him and me ;
Let neither find thy grace, for grace is cruelty.
Me first, O kill me first, and cure my woe ;
Then sheath the sword of justice on my foe ;
Or kill him first, for when his name is heard,
He foremost will receive his due reward.
Arcite of Thebes is he, thy mortal foe,
On whom thy grace did liberty bestow ;
But first contracted, that, if ever found
By day or night upon the Athenian ground,
His head should pay the forfeit ; see returned
The perjured knight, his oath and honour scorned :
For this is he, who, with a borrowed name
And proffered service, to thy palace came,
Now called Philostratus ; retained by thee,
A traitor trusted, and in high degree,
Aspiring to the bed of beauteous Emily.
My part remains, from Thebes my birth I own,
And call myself the unhappy Palamon.
Think me not like that man ; since no disgrace
Can force me to renounce the honour of my
      race.
Know me for what I am : I broke thy chain,
Nor promised I thy prisoner to remain :
The love of liberty with life is given,
And life itself the inferior gift of Heaven.
Thus without crime I fled ; but further know,
I, with this Arcite, am thy mortal foe :
Then give me death, since I thy life pursue ;
For safeguard of thyself, death is my due.

More wouldst thou know?   I love bright Emily,
And for her sake and in her sight will die:
But kill my rival too, for he no less
Deserves; and I thy righteous doom will bless,
Assured that what I lose he never shall possess."
To this replied the stern Athenian prince,
And sourly smiled: "In owning your offence
You judge yourself, and I but keep record
In place of law, while you pronounce the word.
Take your desert, the death you have decreed;
I seal your doom, and ratify the deed:
By Mars, the patron of my arms, you die."
  He said; dumb sorrow seized the standers-by.
The Queen, above the rest, by nature good
(The pattern formed of perfect womanhood),
For tender pity wept: when she began,
Through the bright quire the infectious virtue ran.
All dropt their tears, even the contended maid;
And thus among themselves they softly said:
"What eyes can suffer this unworthy sight!
Two youths of royal blood, renowned in fight,
The mastership of Heaven in face and mind,
And lovers, far beyond their faithless kind:
See their wide-streaming wounds; they neither came
From pride of empire nor desire of fame:
Kings fight for kingdoms, madmen for applause;
But love for love alone, that crowns the lover's cause."
This thought, which ever bribes the beauteous kind,
Such pity wrought in every lady's mind,
They left their steeds, and prostrate on the place,
From the fierce King implored the offenders' grace.
  He paused a while, stood silent in his mood
(For yet his rage was boiling in his blood):
But soon his tender mind the impression felt
(As softest metals are not slow to melt,
And pity soonest runs in gentle minds).
Then reasons with himself; and first he finds
His passion cast a mist before his sense,
And either made or magnified the offence.   [cause?
Offence? Of what? To whom? Who judged the
The prisoner freed himself by nature's laws;

Born free, he sought his right ; the man he freed
Was perjured, but his love excused the deed :
Thus pondering, he looked under with his eyes,
And saw the women's tears, and heard their cries,
Which moved compassion more ; he shook his head,
And softly sighing to himself, he said :
  " Curse on the unpardoning prince, whom tears
    can draw
To no remorse, who rules by lion's law ;
And deaf to prayers, by no submission bowed,
Rends all alike, the penitent and proud !"
At this with look serene he raised his head ;
Reason resumed her place, and passion fled :
Then thus aloud he spoke: "The power of Love,
In earth, and seas, and air, and heaven above,
Rules, unresisted, with an awful nod,
By daily miracles declared a god ;
He blinds the wise, gives eyesight to the blind ;
And moulds and stamps anew the lover's mind.
Behold that Arcite, and this Palamon,
Freed from my fetters, and in safety gone,
What hindered either in their native soil
At ease to reap the harvest of their toil ?
But Love, their lord, did otherwise ordain,
And brought them, in their own despite again,
To suffer death deserved ; for well they know
'Tis in my power, and I their deadly foe.
The proverb holds, that to be wise and love
Is hardly granted to the gods above.
See how the madmen bleed ! behold the gains
With which their master, Love, rewards their pains!
For seven long years on duty every day,
Lo ! their obedience, and their monarch's pay !
Yet, as in duty bound, they serve him on ;
And ask the fools, they think it wisely done ;
Nor ease nor wealth nor life itself regard,
For 'tis their maxim, love is love's reward.
This is not all ; the fair, for whom they strove,
Nor knew before, nor could suspect their love,
Nor thought, when she beheld the fight from far,
Her beauty was the occasion of the war.

But sure a general doom on man is past,
And all are fools and lovers, first or last:
This both by others and myself I know,
For I have served their sovereign long ago;
Oft have been caught within the winding train
Of female snares, and felt the lover's pain,
And learned how far the god can human hearts
    constrain.
To this remembrance, and the prayers of those
Who for the offending warriors interpose,
I give their forfeit lives, on this accord,
To do me homage as their sovereign lord;
And as my vassals, to their utmost might,
Assist my person and assert my right."
This freely sworn, the knights their grace obtained;
Then thus the King his secret thought explained:
" If wealth or honour or a royal race,
Or each or all, may win a lady's grace,
Then either of you knights may well deserve
A princess born; and such is she you serve:
For Emily is sister to the crown,
And but too well to both her beauty known:
But should you combat till you both were dead,
Two lovers cannot share a single bed.
As, therefore, both are equal in degree,
The lot of both be left to destiny.
Now hear the award, and happy may it prove
To her, and him who best deserves her love.
Depart from hence in peace, and free as air,
Search the wide world, and where you please
    repair;
But on the day when this returning sun
To the same point through every sign has run,
Then each of you his hundred knights shall bring
In royal lists, to fight before the King;
And then the knight, whom Fate or happy chance
Shall with his friends to victory advance,
And grace his arms so far in equal fight,
From out the bars to force his opposite,
Or kill, or make him recreant on the plain,
The prize of valour and of love shall gain;

The vanquished party shall their claim release,
And the long jars conclude in lasting peace.
The charge be mine to adorn the chosen ground,
The theatre of war, for champions so renowned;
And take the patron's place of either knight,
With eyes impartial to behold the fight;
And Heaven of me so judge as I shall judge aright.
If both are satisfied with this accord,
Swear by the laws of knighthood on my sword."
   Who now but Palamon exults with joy?
And ravished Arcite seems to touch the sky.
The whole assembled troop was pleased as well,
Extolled the award, and on their knees they fell
To bless the gracious King. The knights, with leave
Departing from the place, his last commands receive,
On Emily with equal ardour look,
And from her eyes their inspiration took:
From thence to Thebes' old walls pursue their way,
Each to provide his champions for the day.
   It might be deemed, on our historian's part,
Or too much neligence or want of art,
If he forgot the vast magnificence
Of royal Theseus, and his large expense.
He first enclosed for lists a level ground,
The whole circumference a mile around;
The form was circular; and all without
A trench was sunk, to moat the place about.
Within, an amphitheatre appeared,
Raised in degrees, to sixty paces reared:
That when a man was placed in one degree,
Height was allowed for him above to see.
   Eastward was built a gate of marble white;
The like adorned the western opposite.
A nobler object than this fabric was
Rome never saw, nor of so vast a space:
For, rich with spoils of many a conquered land,
All arts and artists Theseus could command,
Who sold for hire, or wrought for better fame;
The master-painters and the carvers came.
So rose within the compass of the year
An age's work, a glorious theatre.

Then o'er its eastern gate was raised above
A temple, sacred to the Queen of Love ;
An altar stood below ; on either hand
A priest with roses crowned, who held a myrtle
    wand.
  The dome of Mars was on the gate opposed,
And on the north a turret was enclosed
Within the wall of alabaster white
And crimson coral, for the Queen of Night,
Who takes in sylvan sports her chaste delight.
  Within these oratories might you see
Rich carvings, portraitures, and imagery ;
Where every figure to the life expressed
The godhead's power to whom it was addressed.
In Venus' temple on the sides were seen
The broken slumbers of enamoured men ;
Prayers that even spoke, and pity seemed to call,
And issuing sighs that smoked along the wall ;
Complaints and hot desires, the lover's hell,
And scalding tears that wore a channel where they
And all around were nuptial bonds, the ties   [fell ;
Of love's assurance, and a train of lies,
That, made in lust, conclude in perjuries ;
Beauty, and Youth, and Wealth and Luxury,
And sprightly Hope, and short-enduring Joy,
And Sorceries, to raise the infernal powers,
And Sigils framed in planetary hours ;
Expense, and After-thought, and idle Care,
And Doubts of motley hue, and dark Despair ;
Suspicions and fantastical Surmise,
And Jealousy suffused, with jaundice in her eyes,
Discolouring all she viewed, in tawny dressed,
Down-looked, and with a cuckoo on her fist.
Opposed to her, on the other side advance
The costly feast, the carol, and the dance,
Minstrels and music, poetry and play,
And balls by night, and tournaments by day.
All these were painted on the wall, and more ;
With acts and monuments of times before;
And others added by prophetic doom,
And lovers yet unborn, and loves to come :

For there the Idalian mount, and Cytheron,
The court of Venus, was in colours drawn ;
Before the palace gate, in careless dress
And loose array, sat Portress Idleness ;
There by the fount Narcissus pined alone ;
There Samson was ; with wiser Solomon,
And all the mighty names by love undone.
Medea's charms were there ; Circean feasts,
With bowls that turned enamoured youths to beasts.
Here might be seen, that beauty, wealth, and wit,
And prowess to the power of love submit ;
The spreading snare for all mankind is laid,
And lovers all betray and are betrayed.
The goddess self some noble hand had wrought ;
Smiling she seemed, and full of pleasing thought ;
From ocean as she first began to rise,
And smoothed the ruffled seas and cleared the skies,
She trod the brine, all bare below the breast,
And the green waves but ill-concealed the rest :
A lute she held ; and on her head was seen
A wreath of roses red and myrtles green ;
Her turtles fanned the buxom air above ;
And by his mother stood an infant Love,
With wings unfledged ; his eyes were banded o'er,
His hands a bow, his back a quiver bore,
Supplied with arrows bright and keen, a deadly
      store.
   But in the dome of mighty Mars the red
With different figures all the sides were spread ;
This temple, less in form, with equal grace,
Was imitative of the first in Thrace ;
For that cold region was the loved abode
And sovereign mansion of the warrior god.
The landscape was a forest wide and bare,
Where neither beast nor human kind repair,
The fowl that scent afar the borders fly,
And shun the bitter blast, and wheel about the sky.
A cake of scurf lies baking on the ground,
And prickly stubs, instead of trees, are found ;
Or woods with knots and knares deformed and old,
Headless the most, and hideous to behold :

A rattling tempest through the branches went,
That stripped them bare, and one sole way they bent.
Heaven froze above severe, the clouds congeal,
And through the crystal vault appeared the stand-
    ing hail.
Such was the face without : a mountain stood
Threatening from high, and overlooked the wood :
Beneath the lowering brow, and on a bent,
The temple stood of Mars armipotent ;
The frame of burnished steel, that cast a glare
From far, and seemed to thaw the freezing air.
A straight long entry to the temple led,
Blind with high walls, and horror overhead ;
Thence issued such a blast, and hollow roar,
As threatened from the hinge to heave the door ;
In through that door a northern light there shone ;
'Twas all it had, for windows there were none.
The gate was adamant, eternal frame,
Which, hewed by Mars himself, from Indian
    quarries came,
The labour of a god ; and all along
Tough iron plates were clenched to make it strong.
A tun about was every pillar there ;
A polished mirror shone not half so clear.
There saw I how the secret felon wrought,
And treason labouring in the traitor's thought,
And midwife Time the ripened plot to murder
    brought.
There the red Anger dared the pallid Fear ;
Next stood Hypocrisy, with holy leer,
Soft, smiling, and demurely looking down,
But hid the dagger underneath the gown ;
The assassinating wife, the household fiend ;
And far the blackest there, the traitor-friend.
On the other side there stood Destruction bare,
Unpunished Rapine, and a waste of war ;
Contest with sharpened knives in cloisters drawn,
And all with blood bespread the holy lawn.
Loud menaces were heard, and foul disgrace,
And bawling infamy, in language base ;   [place.
Till sense was lost in sound, and silence fled the

The slayer of himself yet saw I there,
The gore congealed was clotted in his hair;
With eyes half-closed and gaping mouth he lay,
And grim as when he breathed his sullen soul away.
In midst of all the dome, Misfortune sate,
And gloomy Discontent, and fell Debate,
And Madness laughing in his ireful mood;
And armed Complaint on theft; and cries of blood.
There was the murdered corpse, in covert laid,
And violent death in thousand shapes displayed:
The city to the soldier's rage resigned;
Successless wars, and poverty behind:
Ships burnt in fight, or forced on rocky shores,
And the rash hunter strangled by the boars:
The new-born babe by nurses overlaid;
And the cook caught within the raging fire he made.
All ills of Mars his nature, flame and steel;
The gasping charioteer beneath the wheel
Of his own car; the ruined house that falls
And intercepts her lord betwixt the walls:
The whole division that to Mars pertains,
All trades of death that deal in steel for gains
Were there: the butcher, armourer, and smith,
Who forges sharpened faulchions, or the scythe.
The scarlet Conquest on a tower was placed,
With shouts and soldiers' acclamations graced:
A pointed sword hung threatening o'er his head,
Sustained but by a slender twine of thread.
There saw I Mars his ides, the Capitol,
The seer in vain foretelling Cæsar's fall;
The last Triumvirs, and the wars they move,
And Antony, who lost the world for love.
These, and a thousand more, the fane adorn;
Their fates were painted ere the men were born,
All copied from the heavens, and ruling force
Of the red star, in his revolving course.
The form of Mars high on a chariot stood,
All sheathed in arms, and gruffly looked the god;
Two geomantic figures were displayed
Above his head, a warrior and a maid,
One when direct, and one when retrograde.

Tired with deformities of death, I haste
To the third temple of Diana chaste.
A sylvan scene with various greens was drawn,
Shades on the sides, and on the midst a lawn ;
The silver Cynthia, with her nymphs around,
Pursued the flying deer, the woods with horns
Calisto there stood manifest of shame,   [resound ;
And, turned a bear, the northern star became :
Her son was next, and, by peculiar grace,
In the cold circle held the second place ;
The stag Actæon in the stream had spied
The naked huntress, and for seeing died ;
His hounds, unknowing of his change, pursue
The chase, and their mistaken master slew.
Peneian Daphne too was there to see,
Apollo's love before, and now his tree.
The adjoining fane the assembled Greeks expressed,
And hunting of the Calydonian beast.
Œnides' valour, and his envied prize ;
The fatal power of Atalanta's eyes ;
Diana's vengeance on the victor shown,
The murderess mother, and consuming son ;
The Volscian queen extended on the plain,
The treason punished, and the traitor slain.
The rest were various huntings, well designed,
And savage beasts destroyed, of every kind.
The graceful goddess was arrayed in green ;
About her feet were little beagles seen,
That watched with upward eyes the motions of
        their queen.
Her legs were buskined, and the left before,
In act to shoot ; a silver bow she bore,
And at her back a painted quiver wore.
She trod a waxing moon, that soon would wane,
And, drinking borrowed light, be filled again ;
With downcast eyes, as seeming to survey
The dark dominions, her alternate sway.
Before her stood a woman in her throes,
And called Lucina's aid, her burden to disclose.
All these the painter drew with such command,
That nature snatched the pencil from his hand,

C

Ashamed and angry that his art could feign,
And mend the tortures of a mother's pain.
Theseus beheld the fanes of every god,
And thought his mighty cost was well bestowed.
So princes now their poets should regard ;
But few can write, and fewer can reward.
   The theatre thus raised, the lists enclosed,
And all with vast magnificence disposed,
We leave the monarch pleased, and haste to bring
The knights to combat, and their arms to sing.

BOOK III.

THE day approached when Fortune should decide
The important enterprise, and give the bride ;
For now the rivals round the world had sought,
And each his number, well appointed, brought.
The nations far and near contend in choice,
And send the flower of war by public voice ;
That after or before were never known
Such chiefs, as each an army seemed alone.
Beside the champions, all of high degree,
Who knighthood loved, and deeds of chivalry,
Thronged to the lists, and envied to behold
The names of others, not their own, enrolled.
Nor seems it strange ; for every noble knight
Who loves the fair, and is endued with might,
In such a quarrel would be proud to fight.
There breathes not scarce a man on British ground
(An isle for love and arms of old renowned)
But would have sold his life to purchase fame,
To Palamon or Arcite sent his name ;
And had the land selected of the best,
Half had come hence, and let the world provide
   the rest.
A hundred knights with Palamon there came,
Approved in fight, and men of mighty name ;
Their arms were several, as their nations were,
But furnished all alike with sword and spear.

Some wore coat armour, imitating scale,
And next their skins were stubborn shirts of mail :
Some wore a breastplate and a light jupon,
Their horses clothed with rich caparison ;
Some for defence would leathern bucklers use
Of folded hides, and others shields of Pruce.
One hung a pole-axe at his saddle-bow,
And one a heavy mace to stun the foe ;
One for his legs and knees provided well,
With jambeux armed, and double plates of steel :
This on his helmet wore a lady's glove,
And that a sleeve embroidered by his love.

   With Palamon above the rest in place,
Lycurgus came, the surly king of Thrace ;
Black was his beard, and manly was his face,
The balls of his broad eyes rolled in his head,
And glared betwixt a yellow and a red ;
He looked a lion with a gloomy stare,
And o'er his eyebrows hung his matted hair ;
Big-boned and large of limbs, with sinews strong,
Broad-shouldered, and his arms were round and
    long.
Four milk-white bulls (the Thracian use of old)
Were yoked to draw his car of burnished gold.
Upright he stood, and bore aloft his shield,
Conspicuous from afar, and overlooked the field.
His surcoat was a bearskin on his back ;
His hair hung long behind, and glossy raven-black ;
His ample forehead bore a coronet,
With sparkling diamonds and with rubies set.
Ten brace, and more, of greyhounds, snowy fair,
And tall as stags, ran loose, and coursed around
    his chair,
A match for pards in flight, in grappling for the bear ;
With golden muzzles all their mouths were bound,
And collars of the same their necks surround.
Thus through the fields Lycurgus took his way ;
His hundred knights attend in pomp and proud
    array.
   To match this monarch, with strong Arcite came
Emetrius, king of Inde, a mighty name,

On a bay courser, goodly to behold,
The trappings of his horse embossed with barbarous
    gold.
Not Mars bestrode a steed with greater grace;
His surcoat o'er his arms was cloth of Thrace,
Adorned with pearls, all orient, round, and great;
His saddle was of gold, with emeralds set;
His shoulders large a mantle did attire,
With rubies thick, and sparkling as the fire;
His amber-coloured locks in ringlets run,
With graceful negligence, and shone against the sun.
His nose was aquiline, his eyes were blue,
Ruddy his lips, and fresh and fair his hue;
Some sprinkled freckles on his face were seen,
Whose dusk set off the whiteness of the skin.
His awful presence did the crowd surprise,
Nor durst the rash spectator meet his eyes;
Eyes that confessed him born for kingly sway,
So fierce, they flashed intolerable day.
His age in nature's youthful prime appeared,
And just began to bloom his yellow beard.
Whene'er he spoke, his voice was heard around,
Loud as a trumpet, with a silver sound;
A laurel wreathed his temples, fresh and green,
And myrtle sprigs, the marks of love, were mixed
    between.
Upon his fist he bore, for his delight,
An eagle well reclaimed, and lily white.
    His hundred knights attend him to the war,
All armed for battle; save their heads were bare.
Words and devices blazed on every shield,
And pleasing was the terror of the field.
For kings, and dukes, and barons you might see,
Like sparkling stars, though different in degree,
All for the increase of arms, and love of chivalry.
Before the King tame leopards led the way,
And troops of lions innocently play.
So Bacchus through the conquered Indies rode,
And beasts in gambols frisked before their honest
    In this array the war of either side   [god.
Through Athens passed with military pride.

At prime, they entered on the Sunday morn ;
Rich tapestry spread the streets, and flowers the
The town was all a jubilee of feasts ; [posts adorn.
So Theseus willed in honour of his guests ;
Himself with open arms the kings embraced,
Then all the rest in their degrees were graced.
No harbinger was needful for the night,
For every house was proud to lodge a knight.
    I pass the royal treat, nor must relate
The gifts bestowed, nor how the champions sate ;
Who first, who last, or how the knights addressed
Their vows, or who was fairest at the feast ;
Whose voice, whose graceful dance did most surprise,
Soft amorous sighs, and silent love of eyes.
The rivals call my Muse another way,
To sing their vigils for the ensuing day.
'Twas ebbing darkness, past the noon of night ;
And Phosphor, on the confines of the light,
Promised the sun ; ere day began to spring,
The tuneful lark already stretched her wing,
And flickering on her nest, made short essays to sing,
When wakeful Palamon, preventing day,
Took to the royal lists his early way,
To Venus at her fane, in her own house, to pray.
There, falling on his knees before her shrine,
He thus implored with prayers her power divine :
" Creator Venus, genial power of love,
The bliss of men below, and gods above !
Beneath the sliding sun thou runn'st thy race,
Doth fairest shine, and best become thy place.
For thee the winds their eastern blasts forbear,
Thy month reveals the spring, and opens all the year.
Thee, goddess, thee the storms of winter fly ;
Earth smiles with flowers renewing, laughs the sky,
And birds to lays of love their tuneful notes apply.
For thee the lion loathes the taste of blood,
And roaring hunts his female through the wood ;
For thee the bulls rebellow through the groves,
And tempt the stream, and snuff their absent loves.
'Tis thine, whate'er is pleasant, good, or fair ;
All nature is thy province, life thy care ;

Thou mad'st the world, and dost the world repair.
Thou gladder of the mount of Cytheron,
Increase of Jove, companion of the sun,
If e'er Adonis touched thy tender heart,
Have pity, goddess, for thou know'st the smart!
Alas! I have not words to tell my grief;
To vent my sorrow would be some relief;
Light sufferings give us leisure to complain;
We groan, but cannot speak, in greater pain.
O goddess, tell thyself what I would say!
Thou know'st it, and I feel too much to pray.
So grant my suit, as I enforce my might,
In love to be thy champion and thy knight,
A servant to thy sex, a slave to thee,
A foe professed to barren chastity.
Nor ask I fame or honour of the field,
Nor choose I more to vanquish than to yield:
In my divine Emilia make me blest,
Let Fate or partial Chance dispose the rest:
Find thou the manner, and the means prepare;
Possession, more than conquest, is my care.
Mars is the warrior's god; in him it lies
On whom he favours to confer the prize;
With smiling aspect you serenely move
In your fifth orb, and rule the realm of love.
The Fates but only spin the coarser clue,
The finest of the wool is left for you:
Spare me but one small portion of the twine,
And let the Sisters cut below your line:
The rest among the rubbish may they sweep,
Or add it to the yarn of some old miser's heap.
But if you this ambitious prayer deny,
(A wish, I grant, beyond mortality,)
Then let me sink beneath proud Arcite's arms,
And, I once dead, let him possess her charms."
    Thus ended he; then, with observance due,
The sacred incense on her altar threw:
The curling smoke mounts heavy from the fires;
At length it catches flame, and in a blaze expires;
At once the gracious goddess gave the sign,
Her statue shook, and trembled all the shrine:

Pleased Palamon the tardy omen took ;
For since the flames pursued the trailing smoke,
He knew his boon was granted, but the day
To distance driven, and joy adjourned with long
    delay.
   Now morn with rosy light had streaked the sky,
Up rose the sun, and up rose Emily ;
Addressed her early steps to Cynthia's fane,
In state attended by her maiden train,
Who bore the vests that holy rites require,
Incense, and odorous gums, and covered fire.
The plenteous horns with pleasant mead they crown,
Nor wanted aught besides in honour of the moon.
Now, while the temple smoked with hallowed steam,
They wash the virgin in a living stream ;
The secret ceremonies I conceal,
Uncouth, perhaps unlawful to reveal :
But such they were as pagan use required,
Performed by women when the men retired,
Whose eyes profane their chaste mysterious rites
Might turn to scandal or obscene delights.
Well-meaners think no harm ; but for the rest,
Things sacred they pervert, and silence is the best.
Her shining hair, uncombed, was loosely spread,
A crown of mastless oak adorned her head :
When to the shrine approached, the spotless maid
Had kindling fires on either altar laid
(The rites were such as were observed of old,
By Statius in his Theban story told).
Then kneeling with her hands across her breast,
Thus lowly she preferred her chaste request.
   " O goddess, haunter of the woodland green,
To whom both heaven and earth and seas are seen,
Queen of the nether skies, where half the year
Thy silver beams descend, and light the gloomy
    sphere ;
Goddess of maids, and conscious of our hearts,
So keep me from the vengeance of thy darts
(Which Niobe's devoted issue felt,
When hissing through the skies the feathered deaths
    were dealt),

As I desire to live a virgin life,
Nor know the name of mother or of wife.
Thy votress from my tender years I am,
And love, like thee, the woods and sylvan game.
Like death, thou know'st, I loathe the nuptial state,
And man, the tyrant of our sex, I hate,
A lowly servant, but a lofty mate;
Where love is duty on the female side,
On theirs mere sensual gust, and sought with surly
　　pride.
Now by thy triple shape, as thou art seen
In heaven, earth, hell, and everywhere a queen,
Grant this my first desire; let discord cease,
And make betwixt the rivals lasting peace:
Quench their hot fire, or far from me remove
The flame, and turn it on some other love;
Or if my frowning stars have so decreed,
That one must be rejected, one succeed,
Make him my lord, within whose faithful breast
Is fixed my image, and who loves me best.
But oh! even that avert! I choose it not,
But take it as the least unhappy lot.
A maid I am, and of thy virgin train;
Oh, let me still that spotless name retain,
Frequent the forests, thy chaste will obey,
And only make the beasts of chase my prey!"
　　The flames ascend on either altar clear,
While thus the blameless maid addressed her prayer.
When lo! the burning fire that shone so bright
Flew off, all sudden, with extinguished light,
And left one altar dark, a little space,
Which turned self-kindled, and renewed the blaze;
That other victor-flame a moment stood,
Then fell, and lifeless left the extinguished wood;
For ever lost, the irrevocable light
Forsook the blackening coals, and sunk to night:
At either end it whistled as it flew,
And as the brands were green, so dropped the dew,
Infected as it fell with sweat of sanguine hue.
　　The maid from that ill omen turned her eyes,
And with loud shrieks and clamours rent the skies;

Nor knew what signified the boding sign,
But found the powers displeased, and feared the
    wrath divine.
    Then shook the sacred shrine, and sudden light
Sprung through the vaulted roof, and made the
    temple bright.
The Power, behold! the Power in glory shone,
By her bent bow and her keen arrows known;
The rest, a huntress issuing from the wood,
Reclining on her cornel spear she stood.
Then gracious thus began: " Dismiss thy fear,
And Heaven's unchanged decrees attentive hear:
More powerful gods have torn thee from my side,
Unwilling to resign, and doomed a bride;
The two contending knights are weighed above;
One Mars protects, and one the Queen of Love:
But which the man is in the Thunderer's breast;
This he pronounced, '"Tis he who loves thee best.'
The fire that, once extinct, revived again,
Foreshows the love allotted to remain.
Farewell!" she said, and vanished from the place;
The sheaf of arrows shook, and rattled in the case.
Aghast at this, the royal virgin stood,
Disclaimed, and now no more a sister of the wood:
But to the parting goddess thus she prayed:
" Propitious still, be present to my aid,
Nor quite abandon your once favoured maid."
Then sighing she returned; but smiled betwixt,
With hopes, and fears, and joys with sorrows mixt.
    The next returning planetary hour
Of Mars, who shared the heptarchy of power,
His steps bold Arcite to the temple bent,
To adorn with pagan rites the power armipotent:
Then prostrate, low before his altar lay,
And raised his manly voice, and thus began to
    pray:
" Strong god of arms, whose iron sceptre sways
The freezing North, and Hyperborean seas,
And Scythian colds, and Thracia's wintry coast,
Where stand thy steeds, and thou art honoured
    most:

There most, but everywhere thy power is known,
The fortune of the fight is all thy own :
Terror is thine, and wild amazement, flung
From out thy chariot, withers e'en the strong ;
And disarray and shameful rout ensue,
And force is added to the fainting crew.
Acknowledged as thou art, accept my prayer !
If aught I have achieved deserve thy care,
If to my utmost power with sword and shield
I dared the death, unknowing how to yield,
And falling in my rank, still kept the field ;
Then let my arms prevail, by thee sustained,
That Emily by conquest may be gained.
Have pity on my pains ; nor those unknown
To Mars, which, when a lover, were his own.
Venus, the public care of all above,
Thy stubborn heart has softened into love :
Now by her blandishments and powerful charms,
When yielded she lay curling in thy arms,
Even by thy shame, if shame if may be called,
When Vulcan had thee in his net enthralled ;
O envied ignominy, sweet disgrace,
When every god that saw thee wished thy place !
By those dear pleasures, aid my arms in fight,
And make me conquer in my patron's right :
For I am young, a novice in the trade,
The fool of love, unpractised to persuade,
And want the soothing arts that catch the fair,
But, caught myself, lie struggling in the snare ;
And she I love or laughs at all my pain,
Or knows her worth too well, and pays me with
For sure I am, unless I win in arms,   [disdain.
To stand excluded from Emilia's charms :
Nor can my strength avail, unless by thee
Endued with force I gain the victory ;
Then for the fire which warmed thy generous heart,
Pity thy subject's pains and equal smart.
So be the morrow's sweat and labour mine,
The palm and honour of the conquest thine :
Then shall the war, and stern debate, and strife
Immortal, be the business of my life ;

And in thy fane, the dusty spoils among,
High on the burnished roof my banner shall be
    hung,
Ranked with my champion's bucklers; and below,
With arms reversed, the achievements of my foe;
And while these limbs the vital spirit feeds,
While day to night and night to day succeeds,
Thy smoking altar shall be fat with food
Of incense and the grateful steam of blood;
Burnt-offerings morn and evening shall be thine,
And fires eternal in thy temple shine.
The bush of yellow beard, this length of hair,
Which from my birth inviolate I bear,
Guiltless of steel, and from the razor free,
Shall fall a plenteous crop, reserved for thee.
So may my arms with victory be blest,
I ask no more; let Fate dispose the rest."
    The champion ceased; there followed in the close
A hollow groan; a murmuring wind arose;
The rings of iron, that on the doors were hung,
Sent out a jarring sound, and harshly rung:
The bolted gates flew open at the blast,
The storm rushed in, and Arcite stood aghast:
The flames were blown aside, yet shone they bright,
Fanned by the wind, and gave a ruffled light.
    Then from the ground a scent began to rise,
Sweet-smelling as accepted sacrifice:
This omen pleased, and as the flames aspire,
With odorous incense Arcite heaps the fire:
Nor wanted hymns to Mars or heathen charms:
At length the nodding statue clashed his arms,
And with a sullen sound and feeble cry,
Half sung and half pronounced the word of Victory.
For this, with soul devout, he thanked the god,
And, of success secure, returned to his abode.
    These vows, thus granted, raised a strife above
Betwixt the god of war and queen of love.
She, granting first, had right of time to plead;
But he had granted too, nor would recede.
Jove was for Venus, but he feared his wife,
And seemed unwilling to decide the strife;

Till Saturn from his leaden throne arose,
And found a way the difference to compose:
Though sparing of his grace, to mischief bent,
He seldom does a good with good intent.
Wayward, but wise, by long experience taught,
To please both parties, for ill ends, he sought:
For this advantage age from youth has won,
As not to be outridden, though outrun.
By fortune he was now to Venus trined,
And with stern Mars in Capricorn was joined:
Of him disposing in his own abode,
He soothed the goddess, while he gulled the god:
" Cease, daughter, to complain, and stint the strife;
Thy Palamon shall have his promised wife:
And Mars, the lord of conquest, in the fight
With palm and laurel shall adorn his knight.
Wide is my course, nor turn I to my place
Till length of time, and move with tardy pace.
Man feels me, when I press the ethereal plains;
My hand is heavy, and the wound remains.
Mine is the shipwreck in a watery sign;
And in an earthy the dark dungeon mine.
Cold shivering agues, melancholy care,
And bitter blasting winds, and poisoned air,
Are mine, and wilful death, resulting from despair.
The throttling quinsey 'tis my star appoints,
And rheumatisms I send to rack the joints:
When churls rebel against their native prince,
I arm their hands, and furnish the pretence;
And housing in the lion's hateful sign,
Bought senates and deserting troops are mine.
Mine is the privy poisoning; I command
Unkindly seasons and ungrateful land.
By me kings' palaces are pushed to ground,
And miners crushed beneath their mines are found.
'Twas I slew Samson, when the pillared hall
Fell down, and crushed the many with the fall.
My looking is the sire of pestilence,
That sweeps at once the people and the prince.
Now weep no more, but trust thy grandsire's art,
Mars shall be pleased, and thou perform thy part.

'Tis ill, though different your complexions are,
The family of Heaven for men should war."
The expedient pleased, where neither lost his right ;
Mars had the day, and Venus had the night.
The management they left to Chronos' care.
Now turn we to the effect, and sing the war.

In Athens all was pleasure, mirth, and play,
All proper to the spring, and sprightly May,
Which every soul inspired with such delight,
'Twas justing all the day, and love at night :
Heaven smiled, and gladded was the heart of man ;
And Venus had the world as when it first began.
At length in sleep their bodies they compose,
And dreamt the future fight, and early rose.

Now scarce the dawning day began to spring,
As at a signal given, the streets with clamours ring :
At once the crowd arose ; confused and high,
Even from the heaven was heard a shouting cry,
For Mars was early up, and roused the sky.
The gods came downward to behold the wars,
Sharpening their sights, and leaning from their stars.
The neighing of the generous horse was heard,
For battle by the busy groom prepared :
Rustling of harness, rattling of the shield,
Clattering of armour, furbished for the field.
Crowds to the castle mounted up the street ;
Battering the pavement with their coursers' feet :
The greedy sight might there devour the gold
Of glittering arms, too dazzling to behold,
And polished steel that cast the view aside,
And crested morions, with their plumy pride.
Knights, with a long retinue of their squires,
In gaudy liveries march, and quaint attires.
One laced the helm, another held the lance ;
A third the shining buckler did advance.
The courser pawed the ground with restless feet,
And snorting foamed, and champed the golden bit.
The smiths and armourers on palfreys ride,
Files in their hands, and hammers at their side,
And nails for loosened spears and thongs for shields
    provide.

The yeomen guard the streets in seemly bands ;
And clowns come crowding on with cudgels in their
    hands.
  The trumpets, next the gate, in order placed,
Attend the sign to sound the martial blast :
The palace yard is filled with floating tides,
And the last comers bear the former to the sides.
The throng is in the midst ; the common crew
Shut out, the hall admits the better few.
In knots they stand, or in a rank they walk,
Serious in aspect, earnest in their talk ;
Factious, and favouring this or t'other side,
As their strong fancies and weak reason guide ;
Their wagers back their wishes ; numbers hold
With the fair freckled king, and beard of gold :
So vigorous are his eyes, such rays they cast,
So prominent his eagle's beak is placed.
But most their looks on the black monarch bend ;
His rising muscles and his brawn commend ;
His double-biting axe, and beamy spear,
Each asking a gigantic force to rear,
All spoke as partial favour moved the mind ;
And, safe themselves, at others' cost divined.
  Waked by the cries, the Athenian chief arose,
The knightly forms of combat to dispose ;
And passing through the obsequious guards, he
    sate
Conspicuous on a throne, sublime in state ;
There, for the two contending knights he sent ;
Armed cap-a-pie, with reverence low they bent ;
He smiled on both, and with superior look
Alike their offered adoration took.
The people press on every side to see
Their awful Prince, and hear his high decree.
Then signing to their heralds with his hand,
They gave his orders from their lofty stand.
Silence is thrice enjoined ; then thus aloud
The king-at-arms bespeaks the knights and listen-
    ing crowd :
  " Our sovereign lord has pondered in his mind
The means to spare the blood of gentle kind ;

And of his grace and inborn clemency
He modifies his first severe decree,
The keener edge of battle to rebate,
The troops for honour fighting, not for hate.
He wills, not death should terminate their strife,
And wounds, if wounds ensue, be short of life;
But issues, ere the fight, his dread command,
That slings afar, and poniards hand to hand,
Be banished from the field; that none shall dare
With shortened sword to stab in closer war ;
But in fair combat fight with manly strength,
Nor push with biting point, but strike at length.
The tourney is allowed but one career
Of the tough ash, with the sharp-grinded spear ;
But knights unhorsed may rise from off the plain,
And fight on foot their honour to regain ;
Nor, if at mischief taken, on the ground
Be slain, but prisoners to the pillar bound,
At either barrier placed ; nor, captives made,
Be freed, or armed anew the fight invade :
The chief of either side, bereft of life,
Or yielded to his foe, concludes the strife.
Thus dooms the lord : now valiant knights and
    young,
Fight each his fill, with swords and maces long."
  The herald ends : the vaulted firmament
With loud acclaims and vast applause is rent :
Heaven guard a prince so gracious and so good,
So just, and yet so provident of blood !
This was the general cry. The trumpets sound,
And warlike symphony is heard around.
The march'ng troops through Athens take their way,
The great Earl-marshal orders their array.
The fair from high the passing pomp behold ;
A rain of flowers is from the windows rolled.
The casements are with golden tissue spread,
And horses' hoofs, for earth, on silken tapestry tread.
The King goes midmost, and the rivals ride
In equal rank, and close his either side.
Next after these there rode the royal wife,
With Emily, the cause and the reward of strife.

The following cavalcade, by three and three,
Proceed by titles marshalled in degree.
Thus through the southern gate they take their way,
And at the list arrived ere prime of day.
There, parting from the King, the chiefs divide,
And wheeling east and west, before their many
    ride.
The Athenian monarch mounts his throne on high,
And after him the Queen and Emily :
Next these the kindred of the crown are graced
With nearer seats, and lords by ladies placed.
Scarce were they seated, when with clamours loud
In rushed at once a rude promiscuous crowd,
The guards, and then each other overbare,
And in a moment throng the spacious theatre.
Now changed the jarring noise to whispers low,
As winds forsaking seas more softly blow,
When at the western gate, on which the car
Is placed aloft that bears the god of war,
Proud Arcite entering armed before his train
Stops at the barrier, and divides the plain.
Red was his banner, and displayed abroad
The bloody colours of his patron god.
   At that self moment enters Palamon
The gate of Venus, and the rising sun ;
Waved by the wanton winds, his banner flies,
All maiden white, and shares the people's eyes.
From east to west, look all the world around,
Two troops so matched were never to be found ;
Such bodies built for strength, of equal age,
In stature sized ; so proud an equipage :
The nicest eye could no distinction make,
Where lay the advantage, or what side to take.
   Thus ranged, the herald for the last proclaims
A silence, while they answered to their names :
For so the king decreed, to shun with care
The fraud of musters false, the common bane of war.
The tale was just, and then the gates were closed :
And chief to chief, and troop to troop opposed.
The heralds last retired, and loudly cried,
" The fortune of the field be fairly tried !"

At this the challenger, with fierce defy,
His trumpet sounds; the challenged makes reply:
With clangour rings the field, resounds the vaulted
    sky.
Their vizors closed, their lances in the rest,
Or at the helmet pointed or the crest,
They vanish from the barrier, speed the race,
And spurring see decrease the middle space.
A cloud of smoke envelopes either host,
And all at once the combatants are lost:
Darkling they join adverse, and shock unseen,
Coursers with coursers justling, men with men:
As labouring in eclipse, a while they stay,
Till the next blast of wind restores the day.
They look anew: the beauteous form of fight
Is changed, and war appears a grisly sight.
Two troops in fair array one moment showed,
The next, a field with fallen bodies strowed:
Not half the number in their seats are found;
But men and steeds lie grovelling on the ground.
The points of spears are stuck within the shield,
The steeds without their riders scour the field.
The knights unhorsed, on foot renew the fight;
The glittering faulchions cast a gleaming light;
Hauberks and helms are hewed with many a wound,
Out spins the streaming blood, and dyes the ground.
The mighty maces with such haste descend,
They break the bones, and make the solid armour
    bend.
This thrusts amid the throng with furious force;
Down goes, at once, the horseman and the horse:
That courser stumbles on the fallen steed,
And, floundering, throws the rider o'er his head.
One rolls along, a football to his foes;
One with a broken truncheon deals his blows.
This halting, this disabled with his wound,
In triumph led, is to the pillar bound,
Where by the King's award he must abide:
There goes a captive led on tother side.
By fits they cease, and leaning on the lance,
Take breath a while, and to new fight advance.

Full oft the rivals met, and neither spared
His utmost force, and each forgot to ward :
The head of this was to the saddle bent,
The other backward to the crupper sent :
Both were by turns unhorsed ; the jealous blows
Fall thick and heavy, when on foot they close.
So deep their faulchions bite, that every stroke
Pierced to the quick ; and equal wounds they gave
        and took.
Borne far asunder by the tides of men,
Like adamant and steel they met again.
    So when a tiger sucks the bullock's blood,
A famished lion issuing from the wood
Roars lordly fierce, and challenges the food.
Each claims possession, neither will obey,
But both their paws are fastened on the prey ;
They bite, they tear ; and while in vain they strive,
The swains come armed between, and both to
        distance drive.
    At length, as Fate foredoomed, and all things
By course of time to their appointed end ;   [tend
So when the sun to west was far declined,
And both afresh in mortal battle joined,
The strong Emetrius came in Arcite's aid,
And Palamon with odds was overlaid :
For, turning short, he struck with all his might
Full on the helmet of the unwary knight.
Deep was the wound ; he staggered with the blow,
And turned him to his unexpected foe ;
Whom with such force he struck, he felled him down,
And cleft the circle of his golden crown.
But Arcite's men, who now prevailed in fight,
Twice ten at once surround the single knight ;
O'erpowered at length, they force him to the ground,
Unyielded as he was, and to the pillar bound ;
And King Lycurgus, while he fought in vain
His friend to free, was tumbled on the plain.
    Who now laments but Palamon, compelled
No more to try the fortune of the field,
And, worse than death, to view with hateful eyes
His rival's conquest, and renounce the prize !

The royal judge on his tribunal placed,
Who had beheld the fight from first to last,
Bade cease the war ; pronouncing from on high,
Arcite of Thebes had won the beauteous Emily.
The sound of trumpets to the voice replied,
And round the royal lists the heralds cried,
" Arcite of Thebes has won the beauteous bride ! "
    The people rend the skies with vast applause ;
All own the chief, when Fortune owns the cause.
Arcite is owned even by the gods above,
And conquering Mars insults the Queen of Love.
So laughed he when the rightful Titan failed,
And Jove's usurping arms in heaven prevailed.
Laughed all the powers who favour tyranny,
And all the standing army of the sky.
But Venus with dejected eyes appears,
And weeping on the lists distilled her tears ;
Her will refused, which grieves a woman most,
And, in her champion foiled, the cause of love is lost :
Till Saturn said—" Fair daughter, now be still,
The blustering fool has satisfied his will ;
His boon is given ; his knight has gained the day,
But lost the prize ; the arrears are yet to pay.
Thy hour is come, and mine the care shall be
To please thy knight, and set thy promise free."
    Now while the heralds run the lists around,
And Arcite ! Arcite ! heaven and earth resound,
A miracle (nor less it could be called)
Their joy with unexpected sorrow palled.
The victor knight had laid his helm aside,
Part for his ease, the greater part for pride ;
Bareheaded, popularly low he bowed,
And paid the salutations of the crowd ;
Then spurring, at full speed, ran endlong on
Where Theseus sat on his imperial throne ;
Furious he drove, and upward cast his eye,
Where, next the Queen, was placed his Emily ;
Then passing, to the saddle-bow he bent ;
A sweet regard the gracious virgin lent
(For women, to the brave an easy prey,
Still follow Fortune, where she leads the way) :

Just then from earth sprang out a flashing fire.
By Pluto sent, at Saturn's bad desire :
The startling steed was seized with sudden fright,
And, bounding, o'er the pummel cast the knight ;
Forward he flew, and pitching on his head,
He quivered with his feet, and lay for dead.
Black was his countenance in a little space,
For all the blood was gathered in his face.
Help was at hand : they reared him from the ground,
And from his cumbrous arms his limbs unbound ;
Then lanced a vein, and watched returning breath ;
It came, but clogged with symptoms of his death.
The saddle-bow the noble parts had prest,
All bruised and mortified his manly breast.
Him still entranced, and in a litter laid,
They bore from field, and to his bed conveyed.
At length he waked ; and, with a feeble cry,
The word he first pronounced was Emily.

   Meantime the King, though inwardly he mournèd,
In pomp triumphant to the town returned,
Attended by the chiefs who fought the field,
Now friendly mixed, and in one troop compelled ;
Composed his looks to counterfeited cheer,
And bade them not for Arcite's life to fear.
But that which gladded all the warrior train,
Though most were sorely wounded, none were slain.
The surgeons soon despoiled them of their arms,
And some with salves they cure, and some with
     charms ;
Foment the bruises, and the pains assuage,
And heal their inward hurts with sovereign draughts
The King in person visits all around,   [of sage.
Comforts the sick, congratulates the sound ;
Honours the princely chiefs, rewards the rest,
And holds for thrice three days a royal feast.
None was disgraced ; for falling is no shame,
And cowardice alone is loss of fame.
The venturous knight is from the saddle thrown,
But 'tis the fault of fortune, not his own ;
If crowds and palms the conquering side adorn,
The victor under better stars was born :

The brave man seeks not popular applause,
Nor, overpowered with arms, deserts his cause ;
Unshamed, though foiled, he does the best he can :
Force is of brutes, but honour is of man.
   Thus Theseus smiled on all with equal grace,
And each was set according to his place ;
With ease were reconciled the differing parts,
For envy never dwells in noble hearts.
At length they took their leave, the time expired,
Well pleased, and to their several homes retired.
   Meanwhile, the health of Arcite still impairs ;
From bad proceeds to worse, and mocks the leech's
      cares ;
Swoln is his breast, his inward pains increase ;
All means are used, and all without success.
The clottered blood lies heavy on his heart,
Corrupts, and there remains in spite of art ;
Nor breathing veins nor cupping will prevail ;
All outward remedies and inward fail.
The mould of nature's fabric is destroyed,
Her vessels discomposed, her virtue void :
The bellows of his lungs begins to swell ;
All out of frame is every secret cell,
Nor can the good receive, nor bad expel.
Those breathing organs, thus within opprest,
With venom soon distend the sinews of his breast.
Nought profits him to save abandoned life,
Nor vomit's upward aid, nor downward laxative.
The midmost region battered and destroyed,
When nature cannot work, the effect of art is
      void :
For physic can but mend our crazy state,
Patch an old building, not a new create.
Arcite is doomed to die in all his pride,
Must leave his youth, and yield his beauteous bride,
Gained hardly against right, and unenjoyed.
When 'twas declared all hope of life was past,
Conscience, that of all physic works the last,
Caused him to send for Emily in haste.
With her, at his desire, came Palamon ;
Then, on his pillow raised, he thus begun :

" No language can express the smallest part
Of what I feel, and suffer in my heart,
For you, whom best I love and value most ;
But to your service I bequeath my ghost ;
Which, from this mortal body when untied,
Unseen, unheard, shall hover at your side ;
Nor fright you waking, nor your sleep offend,
But wait officious, and your steps attend.
How I have loved, excuse my faltering tongue,
My spirit's feeble, and my pains are strong :
This I may say, I only grieve to die,
Because I lose my charming Emily.
To die, when Heaven had put you in my power !
Fate could not choose a more malicious hour.
What greater curse could envious Fortune give,
Than just to die when I began to live !
Vain men ! how vanishing a bliss we crave ;
Now warm in love, now withering in the grave !
Never, O never more to see the sun !
Still dark, in a damp vault, and still alone !
This fate is common ; but I lose my breath
Near bliss, and yet not blessed before my death.
Farewell ! but take me dying in your arms ;
'Tis all I can enjoy of all your charms :
This hand I cannot but in death resign ;
Ah, could I live ! but while I live 'tis mine.
I feel my end approach, and thus embraced
Am pleased to die ; but hear me speak my last :
Ah, my sweet foe ! for you, and you alone,
I broke my faith with injured Palamon.
But love the sense of right and wrong confounds ;
Strong love and proud ambition have no bounds.
And much I doubt, should Heaven my life
    prolong,
I should return to justify my wrong ;
For while my former flames remain within,
Repentance is but want of power to sin.
With mortal hatred I pursued his life,
Nor he nor you were guilty of the strife ;
Nor I, but as I loved ; yet all combined,
Your beauty and my impotence of mind,

And his concurrent flame that blew my fire,
For still our kindred souls had one desire,
He had a moment's right in point of time ;
Had I seen first, then his had been the crime.
Fate made it mine, and justified his right ;
Nor holds this earth a more deserving knight
For virtue, valour, and for noble blood,
Truth, honour, all that is comprised in good ;
So help me Heaven, in all the world is none
So worthy to be loved as Palamon.
He loves you too, with such a holy fire,
As will not, cannot, but with life expire :
Our vowed affections both have often tried,
Nor any love but yours could ours divide.
Then, by my love's inviolable band,
By my long suffering and my short command,
If e'er you plight your vows when I am gone,
Have pity on the faithful Palamon."
　　This was his last ; for Death came on amain,
And exercised below his iron reign ;
Then upward to the seat of life he goes ;
Sense fled before him, what he touched he froze :
Yet could he not his closing eyes withdraw,
Though less and less of Emily he saw ;
So, speechless, for a little space he lay ;
Then grasped the hand he held, and sighed his
　　　soul away.
　　But whither went his soul ? let such relate
Who search the secrets of the future state :
Divines can say but what themselves believe ;
Strong proofs they have, but not demonstrative ;
For, were all plain, then all sides must agree,
And faith itself be lost in certainty.
To live uprightly then is sure the best ;
To save ourselves, and not to damn the rest.
The soul of Arcite went where heathens go
Who better live than we, though less they know.
　　In Palamon a manly grief appears ;
Silent he wept, ashamed to show his tears.
Emilia shrieked but once ; and then, oppressed
With sorrow, sunk upon her lover's breast :

Till Theseus in his arms conveyed with care
Far from so sad a sight the swooning fair.
'Twere loss of time her sorrow to relate ;
Ill bears the sex a youthful lover's fate,
When just approaching to the nuptial state :
But, like a low-hung cloud, it rains so fast,
That all at once it falls, and cannot last.
The face of things is changed, and Athens now,
That laughed so late, becomes the scene of woe,
Matrons and maids, both sexes, every state,
With tears lament the knight s untimely fate.
Not greater grief in falling Troy was seen
For Hector's death ; but Hector was not then.
Old men with dust deformed their hoary hair ;
The women beat their breasts, their cheeks they tear.
" Why wouldst thou go?" with one consent they cry,
" When thou hadst gold enough, and Emily?"
   Theseus himself, who should have cheered the
Of others, wanted now the same relief :   [grief
Old Ægeus only could revive his son,
Who various changes of the world had known,
And strange vicissitudes of human fate,
Still altering, never in a steady state :
Good after ill and after pain delight,
Alternate, like the scenes of day and night.
Since every man who lives is born to die,
And none can boast sincere felicity,
With equal mind, what happens, let us bear,
Nor joy, nor grieve too much for things beyond
   our care.
Like pilgrims to the appointed place we tend ;
The world's an inn, and death the journey's end.
Even kings but play, and when their part is done,
Some other, worse or better, mount the throne.
With words like these the crowd was satisfied ;
And so they would have been, had Theseus died.
But he, their King, was labouring in his mind
A fitting place for funeral pomps to find,
Which were in honour of the dead designed.
And, after long debate, at last he found
(As love itself had marked the spot of ground),

That grove for ever green, that conscious laund,
Where he with Palamon fought hand to hand ;
That, where he fed his amorous desires
With soft complaints, and felt his hottest fires,
There other flames might waste his earthly part,
And burn his limbs, where love had burned his heart.
    This once resolved, the peasants were enjoined
Sere-wood, and firs, and doddered oaks to find.
With sounding axes to the grove they go,
Fell, split, and lay the fuel in a row ;
Vulcanian food : a bier is next prepared,
On which the lifeless body should be reared,
Covered with cloth of gold ; on which was laid
The corpse of Arcite, in like robes arrayed.
White gloves were on his hands, and on his head
A wreath of laurel, mixed with myrtle, spread.
A sword keen-edged within his right he held,
The warlike emblem of the conquered field :
Bare was his manly visage on the bier ;
Menaced his countenance, even in death severe.
Then to the palace-hall they bore the knight,
To lie in solemn state, a public sight :
Groans, cries, and howlings fill the crowded place,
And unaffected sorrow sat on every face.
Sad Palamon above the rest appears,
In sable garments, dewed with gushing tears ;
His auburn locks on either shoulder flowed,
Which to the funeral of his friend he vowed ;
But Emily, as chief, was next his side,
A virgin-widow and a mourning bride.
And, that the princely obsequies might be
Performed according to his high degree, ·
The steed, that bore him living to the fight,
Was trapped with polished steel, all shining bright,
And covered with the achievements of the knight.
The riders rode abreast ; and one his shield,
His lance of cornel-wood another held ;
The third his bow, and, glorious to behold,
The costly quiver, all of burnished gold.
The noblest of the Grecians next appear,
And weeping on their shoulders bore the bier ;

With sober pace they marched, and often stayed,
And through the master-street the corpse conveyed.
The houses to their tops with black were spread,
And even the pavements were with mourning hid.
The right side of the pall old Ægeus kept,
And on the left the royal Theseus wept ;
Each bore a golden bowl of work divine,
With honey filled, and milk, and mixed with ruddy
    wine.
Then Palamon, the kinsman of the slain,
And after him appeared the illustrious train.
To grace the pomp came Emily the bright,
With covered fire, the funeral pile to light.
With high devotion was the service made,
And all the rites of pagan honour paid :
So lofty was the pile, a Parthian bow,
With vigour drawn, must send the shaft below.
The bottom was full twenty fathom broad,
With crackling straw beneath in due proportion
    strowed.
The fabric seemed a wood of rising green,
With sulphur and bitumen cast between
To feed the flames : the trees were unctuous fir,
And mountain-ash, the mother of the spear ;
The mourner-yew and builder-oak were there,
The beech, the swimming alder, and the plane,
Hard box, and linden of a softer grain,
And laurels, which the gods for conquering chiefs
    ordain.
How they were ranked shall rest untold by me,
With nameless nymphs that lived in every tree ;
Nor how the dryads and the woodland train,
Disherited, ran howling o'er the plain :
Nor how the birds to foreign seats repaired,
Or beasts that bolted out and saw the forest bared :
Nor how the ground, now cleared, with ghastly fright
Beheld the sudden sun, a stranger to the light.
    The straw, as first I said, was laid below :
Of chips and sere-wood was the second row :
The third of greens, and timber newly felled ;
The fourth high stage the fragrant odours held,

And pearls, and precious stones, and rich array ;
In midst of which, embalmed, the body lay.
The service sung, the maid with mourning eyes
The stubble fired ; the smouldering flames arise :
This office done, she sunk upon the ground ;
But what she spoke, recovered from her swound,
I want the wit in moving words to dress ;
But by themselves the tender sex may guess.
While the devouring fire was burning fast,
Rich jewels in the flame the wealthy cast ;
And some their shields, and some their lances threw,
And gave the warrior's ghost a warrior's due.
Full bowls of wine, of honey, milk and blood,
Were poured upon the pile of burning wood,
And hissing flames receive, and hungry lick the food.
Then thrice the mounted squadrons ride around
The fire, and Arcite's name they thrice resound :
" Hail and farewell !" they shouted thrice amain,
Thrice facing to the left, and thrice they turned
    again :
Still, as they turned, they beat their clattering shields;
The women mix their cries, and clamour fills the
    fields.
The warlike wakes continued all the night,
And funeral games were played at new returning
    light :
Who naked wrestled best, besmeared with oil,
Or who with gauntlets gave or took the foil,
I will not tell you, nor would you attend ;
But briefly haste to my long story's end.
  I pass the rest ; the year was fully mourned,
And Palamon long since to Thebes returned ;
When by the Grecians' general consent,
At Athens Theseus held his parliament ;
Among the laws that passed, it was decreed,
That conquered Thebes from bondage should be
    freed ;
Reserving homage to the Athenian throne,
To which the sovereign summoned Palamon.
Unknowing of the cause, he took his way,
Mournful in mind, and still in black array.

The monarch mounts the throne, and, placed on
    high,
Commands into the court the beauteous Emily.
So called, she came; the senate rose, and paid
Becoming reverence to the royal maid.
And first, soft whispers through the assembly went;
With silent wonder then they watched the event;
All hushed, the King arose with awful grace;
Deep thought was in his breast, and counsel in his
    face:
At length he sighed, and having first prepared
The attentive audience, thus his will declared:
  " The Cause and Spring of motion from above
Hung down on earth the golden chain of love;
Great was the effect, and high was His intent,
When peace among the jarring seeds He sent;
Fire, flood, and earth and air by this were bound,
And love, the common link, the new creation
    crowned.
The chain still holds; for though the forms decay,
Eternal matter never wears away:
The same First Mover certain bounds has placed,
How long those perishable forms shall last;
Nor can they last beyond the time assigned
By that all-seeing and all-making Mind:
Shorten their hours they may, for will is free,
But never pass the appointed destiny.
So men oppressed, when weary of their breath,
Throw off the burden, and suborn their death.
Then, since those forms begin, and have their end,
On some unaltered cause they sure depend:
Parts of the whole are we, but God the whole,
Who gives us life, and animating soul.
For nature cannot from a part derive
That being which the whole can only give:
He perfect, stable; but imperfect we,
Subject to change, and different in degree;
Plants, beasts, and man; and, as our organs are,
We more or less of His perfection share.
But, by a long descent, the ethereal fire
Corrupts; and forms, the mortal part, expire.

As He withdraws His virtue, so they pass,
And the same matter makes another mass:
This law the omniscient Power was pleased to give,
That every kind should by succession live;
That individuals die, His will ordains;
The propagated species still remains.
The monarch oak, the patriarch of the trees,
Shoots rising up, and spreads by slow degrees;
Three centuries he grows, and three he stays,
Supreme in state, and in three more decays:
So wears the paving pebble in the street,
And towns and towers their fatal periods meet:
So rivers, rapid once, now naked lie,
Forsaken of their springs, and leave their channels
　　dry.
So man, at first a drop, dilates with heat,
Then, formed, the little heart begins to beat;
Secret he feeds, unknowing, in the cell;
At length, for hatching ripe, he breaks the shell,
And struggles into breath, and cries for aid;
Then helpless in his mother's lap is laid.
He creeps, he walks, and, issuing into man,
Grudges their life from whence his own began;
Reckless of laws, affects to rule alone,
Anxious to reign, and reckless on the throne;
First vegetive, then feels, and reasons last;
Rich of three souls, and lives all three to waste.
Some thus; but thousands more in flower of age,
For few arrive to run the latter stage.
Sunk in the first, in battle some are slain,
And others whelmed beneath the stormy main.
What makes all this, but Jupiter the king,
At whose command we perish, and we spring?
Then 'tis our best, since thus ordained to die,
To make a virtue of necessity;
Take what he gives, since to rebel is vain;
The bad grows better, which we well sustain;
And could we choose the time, and choose aright,
'Tis best to die, our honour at the height.
When we have done our ancestors no shame,
But served our friends, and well secured our fame;

Then should we wish our happy life to close,
And leave no more for Fortune to dispose ;
So should we make our death a glad relief
From future shame, from sickness, and from grief ;
Enjoying while we live the present hour,
And dying in our excellence and flower.
Then round our deathbed every friend should run,
And joy us of our conquest early won ;
While the malicious world, with envious tears,
Should grudge our happy end, and wish it theirs.
Since then our Arcite is with honour dead,
Why should we mourn, that he so soon is freed,
Or call untimely what the gods decreed ?
With grief as just, a friend may be deplored,
From a foul prison to free air restored.
Ought he to thank his kinsman or his wife,
Could tears recall him into wretched life ?
Their sorrow hurts themselves ; on him is lost,
And worse than both, offends his happy ghost.
What then remains, but after past annoy
To take the good vicissitude of joy ;
To thank the gracious gods for what they give,
Possess our souls, and, while we live, to live ?
Ordain we then two sorrows to combine,
And in one point the extremes of grief to join ;
That thence resulting joy may be renewed,
As jarring notes in harmony conclude.
Then I propose that Palamon shall be
In marriage joined with beauteous Emily ;
For which already I have gained the assent
Of my free people in full parliament.
Long love to her has borne the faithful knight,
And well deserved, had Fortune done him right :
'Tis time to mend her fault, since Emily
By Arcite's death from former vows is free ;
If you, fair sister, ratify the accord,
And take him for your husband and your lord,
'Tis no dishonour to confer your grace
On one descended from a royal race ;
And were he less, yet years of service past
From grateful souls exact reward at last.

Pity is Heaven's and yours ; nor can she find
A throne so soft as in a woman's mind."
He said ; she blushed ; and as o'erawed by might,
Seemed to give Theseus what she gave the knight.
Then, turning to the Theban, thus he said :
"Small arguments are needful to persuade
Your temper to comply with my command : "
And speaking thus, he gave Emilia's hand.
Smiled Venus, to behold her own true knight
Obtain the conquest, though he lost the fight ;
And blessed with nuptial bliss the sweet laborious
Eros and Anteros on either side,   [night.
One fired the bridegroom, and one warmed the bride ;
And long-attending Hymen from above
Showered on the bed the whole Idalian grove.
All of a tenor was their after-life,
No day discoloured with domestic strife ;
No jealousy, but mutual truth believed,
Secure repose, and kindness undeceived.
Thus Heaven, beyond the compass of his thought,
Sent him the blessing he so dearly bought.

So may the Queen of Love long duty bless,
And all true lovers find the same success.

The Cock and the Fox; or, The Tale of the Nun's Priest.

FROM CHAUCER.

THERE lived, as authors tell, in days of yore,
A widow, somewhat old, and very poor :
Deep in a cell her cottage lonely stood,
Well thatched, and under covert of a wood.
  This dowager, on whom my tale I found,
Since last she laid her husband in the ground,
A simple sober life in patience led,
And had but just enough to buy her bread ;
But huswifing the little Heaven had lent,
She duly.paid a groat for quarter-rent ;
And pinched her belly, with her daughters two,
To bring the year about with much ado.
  The cattle in her homestead were three sows,
An ewe called Mally, and three brinded cows.
Her parlour window stuck with herbs around
Of savoury smell ; and rushes strewed the ground.
A maple dresser in her hall she had,
On which full many a slender meal she made,
For no delicious morsel passed her throat ;
According to her cloth she cut her coat ;
No poignant sauce she knew, no costly treat,
Her hunger gave a relish to her meat.
A sparing diet did her health assure ;
Or sick, a pepper posset was her cure.
Before the day was done, her work she sped,
And never went by candle-light to bed.
With exercise she sweat ill humours out ;
Her dancing was not hindered by the gout.

Her poverty was glad, her heart content,
Nor knew she what the spleen or vapours meant.
Of wine she never tasted through the year,
But white and black was all her homely cheer ;
Brown bread, and milk (but first she skimmed her
  bowls),
And rashers of singed bacon on the coals.
On holy days, an egg or two at most ;
But her ambition never reached to roast.
 A yard she had with pales enclosed about,
Some high, some low, and a dry ditch without.
Within this homestead lived, without a peer
For crowing loud, the noble Chanticleer ;
So hight her cock, whose singing did surpass
The merry notes of organs at the mass.
More certain was the crowing of a cock
To number hours, than is an abbey clock ;
And sooner than the matin-bell was rung,
He clapped his wings upon his roost, and sung :
For when degrees fifteen ascended right,
By sure instinct he knew 'twas one at night.
High was his comb, and coral-red withal,
In dents embattled like a castle wall ;
His bill was raven-black, and shone like jet ;
Blue were his legs, and orient were his feet ;
White were his nails, like silver to behold,
His body glittering like the burnished gold.
 This gentle cock, for solace of his life,
Six misses had beside his lawful wife ;
Scandal, that spares no king, though ne'er so good,
Says they were all of his own flesh and blood,
His sisters both by sire and mother's side ;
And sure their likeness showed them near allied.
But make the worst, the monarch did no more
Than all the Ptolemys had done before :
When incest is for interest of a nation,
'Tis made no sin by holy dispensation.
Some lines have been maintained by this alone,
Which by their common ugliness are known.
 But passing this as from our tale apart,
Dame Partlet was the sovereign of his heart :

Ardent in love, outrageous in his play,
He feathered her a hundred times a day ;
And she, that was not only passing fair,
But was withal discreet and debonair,
Resolved the passive doctrine to fulfil,
Though loth, and let him work his wicked will :
At board and bed was affable and kind,
According as their marriage-vow did bind,
And as the Church's precept had enjoined.
Even since she was a sennight old, they say,
Was chaste and humble to her dying day,
Nor chick nor hen was known to disobey.

By this her husband's heart she did obtain ;
What cannot beauty joined with virtue gain?
She was his only joy, and he her pride :
She, when he walked, went pecking by his side ;
If, spurning up the ground, he sprung a corn,
The tribute in his bill to her was borne.
But oh ! what joy it was to hear him sing
In summer, when the day began to spring,
Stretching his neck, and warbling in his throat,
Solus cum sola then was all his note.
For in the days of yore, the birds of parts
Were bred to speak, and sing, and learn the
     liberal arts.

It happed that perching on the parlour beam
Amidst his wives, he had a deadly dream,
Just at the dawn ; and sighed and groaned so fast,
As every breath he drew would be his last.
Dame Partlet, ever nearest to his side,
Heard all his piteous moan, and how he cried
For help from gods and men ; and sore aghast
She pecked and pulled, and wakened him at last.
"Dear heart," said she, "for love of Heaven declare
Your pain, and make me partner in your care.
You groan, sir, ever since the morning light,
As something had disturbed your noble spright."

"And, madam, well I might," said Chanticleer,
"Never was shrovetide-cock in such a fear.
Even still I run all over in a sweat,
My princely senses not recovered yet.

For such a dream I had of dire portent,
That much I fear my body will be shent ;
It bodes I shall have wars and woeful strife,
Or in a loathsome dungeon end my life.
Know, dame, I dreamt within my troubled breast,
That in our yard I saw a murderous beast,
That on my body would have made arrest.
With waking eyes I ne'er beheld his fellow ;
His colour was betwixt a red and yellow :
Tipped was his tail, and both his pricking ears,
With black ; and much unlike his other hairs :
The rest, in shape a beagle's whelp throughout,
With broader forehead, and a sharper snout :
Deep in his front were sunk his glowing eyes,
That yet, methinks, I see him with surprise.
Reach out your hand, I drop with clammy sweat,
And lay it to my heart, and feel it beat."
    " Now fie for shame," quoth she, " by Heaven
Thou hast for ever lost thy lady's love.   [above,
No woman can endure a recreant knight ;
He must be bold by day, and free by night :
Our sex desires a husband or a friend
Who can our honour and his own defend ;
Wise, hardy, secret, liberal of his purse ;
A fool is nauseous, but a coward worse :
No bragging coxcomb, yet no baffled knight.
How darest thou talk of love, and darest not fight ?
How darest thou tell thy dame thou art afeard ?
Hast thou no manly heart, and hast a beard ?
    If aught from fearful dreams may be divined,
They signify a cock of dunghill kind.
All dreams, as in old Galen I have read,
Are from repletion and complexion bred ;
From rising fumes of indigested food,
And noxious humours that infect the blood :
And sure, my lord, if I can read aright,
These foolish fancies you have had to-night
Are certain symptoms (in the canting style)
Of boiling choler and abounding bile ;
This yellow gall that in your stomach floats
Engenders all these visionary thoughts.

When choler overflows, then dreams are bred
Of flames, and all the family of red ;
Red dragons and red beasts in sleep we view,
For humours are distinguished by their hue.
From hence we dream of wars and warlike things,
And wasps and hornets with their double wings.
   Choler adust congeals our blood with fear ;
Then black bulls toss us, and black devils tear.
In sanguine airy dreams aloft we bound ;
With rheums oppressed, we sink in rivers drowned.
   More I could say, but thus conclude my theme,
The dominating humour makes the dream.
Cato was in his time accounted wise,
And he condemns them all for empty lies.
Take my advice, and when we fly to ground,
With laxatives preserve your body sound,
And purge the peccant humours that abound.
I should be loth to lay you on a bier ;
And though there lives no 'pothecary near,
I dare for once prescribe for your disease,
And save long bills and a damned doctor's fees.
   Two sovereign herbs, which I by practice know,
Are both at hand (for in our yard they grow),
On peril of my soul shall rid you wholly
Of yellow choler, and of melancholy :
You must both purge and vomit ; but obey,
And for the love of Heaven make no delay.
Since hot and dry in your complexion join,
Beware the sun when in a vernal sign ;
For when he mounts exalted in the Ram,
If then he finds your body in a flame,
Replete with choler, I dare lay a groat,
A tertian ague is at least your lot.
Perhaps a fever (which the gods forfend)
May bring your youth to some untimely end :
And therefore, sir, as you desire to live,
A day or two before your laxative,
Take just three worms, nor under nor above,
Because the gods unequal numbers love,
These digestives prepare you for your purge ;
Of fumetery, centaury, and spurge,

And of ground-ivy add a leaf or two,
All which within our yard or garden grow.
Eat these, and be, my lord, of better cheer ;
Your father's son was never born to fear."
  "Madam," quoth he, "gramercy for your care,
But Cato, whom you quoted, you may spare ;
'Tis true, a wise and worthy man he seems,
And, as you say, gave no belief to dreams ;
But other men of more authority,
And, by the immortal powers, as wise as he,
Maintain, with sounder sense, that dreams fore-
    bode ;
For Homer plainly says they come from God.
Nor Cato said it ; but some modern fool
Imposed in Cato's name on boys at school.
  Believe me, madam, morning dreams foreshow .
The events of things, and future weal or woe :
Some truths are not by reason to be tried,
But we have sure experience for our guide.
An ancient author, equal with the best,
Relates this tale of dreams among the rest :
  Two friends, or brothers, with devout intent,
On some far pilgrimage together went.
It happened so, that, when the sun was down,
They just arrived by twilight at a town :
That day had been the baiting of a bull,
'Twas at a feast, and every inn so full,
That no void room in chamber or on ground,
And but one sorry bed, was to be found,
And that so little it would hold but one,
Though till this hour they never lay alone.
  So were they forced to part ; one stayed behind,
His fellow sought what lodging he could find ;
At last he found a stall where oxen stood,
And that he rather chose than lie abroad.
'Twas in a farther yard without a door ;
But, for his ease, well littered was the floor.
His fellow, who the narrow bed had kept,
Was weary, and without a rocker slept :
Supine he snored ; but in the dead of night
He dreamt his friend appeared before his sight,

Who, with a ghastly look and doleful cry,
Said, ' Help me, brother, or this night I die :
Arise and help, before all help be vain,
Or in an ox's stall I shall be slain.'
   Roused from his rest, he wakened in a start,
Shivering with horror, and with aching heart :
At length to cure himself by reason tries ;
'Tis but a dream, and what are dreams but lies?
So thinking changed his side, and closed his eyes.
His dream returns ; his friend appears again :
' The murderers come, now help, or I am slain :'
'Twas but a vision still, and visions are but vain.
   He dreamt the third : but now his friend appeared
Pale, naked, pierced with wounds, with blood be-
     smeared :
' Thrice warned, awake,' said he ; ' relief is late,
The deed is done, but thou revenge my fate :
Tardy of aid, unseal thy heavy eyes,
Awake, and with the dawning day arise :
Take to the western gate thy ready way,
For by that passage they my corpse convey :
My corpse is in a tumbril laid, among
The filth and ordure, and enclosed with dung.
That cart arrest, and raise a common cry ;
For sacred hunger of my gold I die :'
Then showed his grisly wounds ; and last he drew
A piteous sigh, and took a long adieu.
The frighted friend arose by break of day,
And found the stall where late his fellow lay.
Then of his impious host inquiring more,
Was answered that his guest was gone before :
' Muttering he went,' said he, ' by morning light,
And much complained of his ill rest by night.'
This raised suspicion in the pilgrim's mind ;
Because all hosts are of an evil kind,
And oft to share the spoil with robbers joined.
   His dream confirmed his thought : with troubled
     look
Straight to the western gate his way he took ;
There as his dream foretold, a cart he found,
That carried compost forth to dung the ground.

This when the pilgrim saw, he stretched his throat,
And cried out ' Murder' with a yelling note.
' My murdered fellow in this cart lies dead ;
Vengeance and justice on the villain's head !
You, magistrates, who sacred laws dispense,
On you I call to punish this offence.'
   The word thus given, within a little space
The mob came roaring out, and thronged the place.
All in a trice they cast the cart to ground,
And in the dung the murdered body found ;
Though breathless, warm and reeking from the
    wound.
Good Heaven, whose darling attribute we find
Is boundless grace and mercy to mankind,
Abhors the cruel ; and the deeds of night
By wondrous ways reveals in open light :
Murder may pass unpunished for a time,
But tardy justice will o'ertake the crime.
And oft a speedier pain the guilty feels,
The hue and cry of heaven pursues him at the
    heels,
Fresh from the fact ; as in the present case,
The criminals are seized upon the place :
Carter and host confronted face to face.
Stiff in denial, as the law appoints,
On engines they distend their tortured joints :
So was confession forced, the offence was known,
And public justice on the offenders done.
   Here may you see that visions are to dread ;
And in the page that follows this, I read
Of two young merchants, whom the hope of gain
Induced in partnership to cross the main ;
Waiting till willing winds their sails supplied,
Within a trading town they long abide,
Full fairly situate on a haven's side.
   One evening it befell, that looking out,
The wind they long had wished was come about ;
Well pleased they went to rest ; and if the gale
Till morn continued, both resolved to sail.
But as together in a bed they lay,
The younger had a dream at break of day.

A man, he thought, stood frowning at his side,
Who warned him for his safety to provide,
Not put to sea, but safe on shore abide.
' I come, thy genius, to command thy stay ;
Trust not the winds, for fatal is the day,
And death unhoped attends the watery way.'
   The vision said, and vanished from his sight ;
The dreamer wakened in a mortal fright ;
Then pulled his drowsy neighbour, and declared
What in his slumber he had seen and heard.
His friend smiled scornful, and, with proud con-
Rejects as idle what his fellow dreamt.   [tempt,
' Stay who will stay ; for me no fears restrain,
Who follow Mercury, the god of gain ;
Let each man do as to his fancy seems,
I wait not, I, till you have better dreams.
Dreams are but interludes, which fancy makes ;
When monarch reason sleeps, this mimic wakes ;
Compounds a medley of disjointed things,
A mob of cobblers and a court of kings :
Light fumes are merry, grosser fumes are sad ;
Both are the reasonable soul run mad ;
And many monstrous forms in sleep we see,
That neither were nor are nor e'er can be.
Sometimes, forgotten things long cast behind
Rush forward in the brain, and come to mind.
The nurse's legends are for truths received,
And the man dreams but what the boy believed.
   Sometimes we but rehearse a former play,
The night restores our actions done by day,
As hounds in sleep will open for their prey.
In short, the farce of dreams is of a piece,
Chimeras all ; and more absurd, or less.
You, who believe in tales, abide alone ;
Whate'er I get, this voyage is my own.'
   Thus while he spoke, he heard the shouting crew
That called aboard, and took his last adieu.
The vessel went before a merry gale,
And for quick passage put on every sail :
But when least feared, and even in open day,
The mischief overtook her in the way :

Whether she sprung a leak, I cannot find,
Or whether she was overset with wind,
Or that some rock below her bottom rent ;
But down at once with all her crew she went.
Her fellow-ships from far her loss descried ;
But only she was sunk, and all were safe beside.
　By this example you are taught again,
That dreams and visions are not always vain :
But if, dear Partlet, you are yet in doubt,
Another tale shall make the former out.
　Kenelm, the son of Kenulph, Mercia's king,
Whose holy life the legends loudly sing,
Warned in a dream, his murder did foretell
From point to point as after it befell ;
All circumstances to his nurse he told
(A wonder from a child of seven years old) ;
The dream with horror heard, the good old wife
From treason counselled him to guard his life ;
But close to keep the secret in his mind,
For a boy's vision small belief would find.
The pious child, by promise bound, obeyed,
Nor was the fatal murder long delayed :
By Quenda slain, he fell before his time,
Made a young martyr by his sister's crime.
The tale is told by venerable Bede,
Which, at your better leisure, you may read.
　Macrobius too relates the vision sent
To the great Scipio, with the famed event ;
Objections makes, but after makes replies,
And adds, that dreams are often prophecies.
　Of Daniel you may read in holy writ,
Who, when the king his vision did forget,
Could word for word the wondrous dream repeat.
Nor less of patriarch Joseph understand,
Who by a dream enslaved the Egyptian land,
The years of plenty and of dearth foretold,
When for their bread their liberty they sold.
Nor must the exalted butler be forgot,
Nor he whose dream presaged his hanging lot.
　And did not Croesus the same death foresee,
Raised in his vision on a lofty tree ?

The wife of Hector, in his utmost pride,
Dreamt of his death the night before he died;
Well was he warned from battle to refrain;
But men to death decreed are warned in vain;
He dared the dream, and by his fatal foe was slain.
  Much more I know, which I forbear to speak,
For see, the ruddy day begins to break:
Let this suffice, that plainly I foresee
My dream was bad, and bodes adversity;
But neither pills nor laxatives I like,
They only serve to make the well man sick:
Of these his gain the sharp physician makes,
And often gives a purge, but seldom takes;
They not correct, but poison all the blood,
And ne'er did any but the doctors good.
Their tribe, trade, trinkets, I defy them all,
With every work of 'Pothecaries Hall.
  These melancholy matters I forbear;
But let me tell thee, Partlet mine, and swear,
That when I view the beauties of thy face,
I fear not death nor dangers nor disgrace;
So may my soul have bliss, as when I spy
The scarlet red about thy partridge eye,
While thou art constant to thy own true knight,
While thou art mine, and I am thy delight,
All sorrows at thy presence take their flight.
For true it is, as *in principio*,
Mulier est hominis confusio.
Madam, the meaning of this Latin is,
That woman is to man his sovereign bliss.
For when by night I feel your tender side,
Though for the narrow perch I cannot ride,
Yet I have such a solace in my mind,
That all my boding cares are cast behind,
And even already I forget my dream."
He said, and downward flew from off the beam,
For daylight now began apace to spring,
The thrush to whistle, and the lark to sing.
Then crowing clapped his wings, the appointed
    call,
To chuck his wives together in the hall.

By this the widow had unbarred the door,
And Chanticleer went strutting out before,
With royal courage, and with heart so light,
As showed he scorned the visions of the night.
Now roaming in the yard, he spurned the ground,
And gave to Partlet the first grain he found.
Then often feathered her with wanton play,
And trod her twenty times ere prime of day;
And took by turns and gave so much delight,
Her sisters pined with envy at the sight.

He chucked again, when other corns he found,
And scarcely deigned to set a foot to ground,
But swaggered like a lord about his hall,
And his seven wives came running at his call.

'Twas now the month in which the world began
(If March beheld the first created man);
And since the vernal equinox, the sun
In Aries twelve degrees or more had run;
When, casting up his eyes against the light,
Both month, and day, and hour, he measured right,
And told more truly than the Ephemeris:
For art may err, but nature cannot miss.

Thus numbering times and seasons in his breast,
His second crowing the third hour confessed.
Then turning, said to Partlet: "See, my dear,
How lavish nature has adorned the year;
How the pale primrose and blue violet spring,
And birds essay their throats disused to sing:
All these are ours; and I with pleasure see
Man strutting on two legs, and aping me:
An unfledged creature of a lumpish frame,
Endued with fewer particles of flame:
Our dame sits cowering o'er a kitchen fire,
I draw fresh air, and Nature's works admire;
And even this day in more delight abound,
Than, since I was an egg, I ever found."

The time shall come when Chanticleer shall wish
His words unsaid, and hate his boasted bliss;
The crested bird shall by experience know,
Jove made not him his masterpiece below,
And learn the latter end of joy is woe.

The vessel of his bliss to dregs is run,
And Heaven will have him taste his other tun.
　　Ye wise, draw near, and hearken to my tale,
Which proves that oft the proud by flattery fall;
The legend is as true, I undertake,
As Tristram is, and Launcelot of the Lake :
Which all our ladies in such reverence hold,
As if in Book of Martyrs it were told.
　　A fox full fraught with seeming sanctity,
That feared an oath, but, like the devil, would lie;
Who looked like Lent, and had the holy leer,
And durst not sin before he said his prayer;
This pious cheat, that never sucked the blood
Nor chawed the flesh of lambs, but when he could,
Had passed three summers in the neighbouring wood:
And musing long whom next to circumvent,
On Chanticleer his wicked fancy bent;
And in his high imagination cast
By stratagem to gratify his taste.
　　The plot contrived, before the break of day
Saint Reynard through the hedge had made his way;
The pale was next, but, proudly, with a bound
He leapt the fence of the forbidden ground :
Yet fearing to be seen, within a bed
Of coleworts he concealed his wily head;
Then skulked till afternoon, and watched his time,
As murderers use, to perpetrate his crime.
　　O hypocrite, ingenious to destroy!
O traitor, worse than Sinon was to Troy!
O vile subverter of the Gallic reign,
More false than Gano was to Charlemagne!
O Chanticleer, in an unhappy hour
Didst thou forsake the safety of thy bower!
Better for thee thou hadst believed thy dream,
And not that day descended from the beam!
　　But here the doctors eagerly dispute;
Some hold predestination absolute;
Some clerks maintain that Heaven at first foresees,
And in the virtue of foresight decrees.
If this be so, then prescience binds the will,
And mortals are not free to good or ill;

For what He first foresaw He must ordain,
Or its eternal prescience may be vain ;
As bad for us as prescience had not been ;
For, first or last, He's author of the sin.
And who says that, let the blaspheming man
Say worse even of the devil, if he can.
For how can that eternal Power be just
To punish man, who sins because he must?
Or, how can He reward a virtuous deed,
Which is not done by us, but first decreed?
   I cannot boult this matter to the bran,
As Bradwardin and holy Austin can :
If prescience can determine actions so
That we must do, because he did foreknow,
Or that foreknowing, yet our choice is free,
Not forced to sin by strict necessity ;
This strict necessity they simple call,
Another sort there is, conditional.
The first so binds the will that things foreknown
By spontaneity, not choice, are done.
Thus galley-slaves tug willing at their oar,
Consent to work, in prospect of the shore,
But would not work at all, if not constrained before.
That other does not liberty constrain,
But man may either act, or may refrain.
Heaven made us agents free to good or ill,
And forced it not, though He foresaw the will.
Freedom was first bestowed on human race,
And prescience only held the second place.
   If He could make such agents wholly free,
I not dispute ; the point's too high for me :
For Heaven's unfathomed power what man can
    sound,
Or put to His omnipotence a bound?
He made us to His image, all agree ;
That image is the soul, and that must be
Or not the Maker's image or be free.
   But whether it were better man had been
By nature bound to good, not free to sin,
I waive, for fear of splitting on a rock.
The tale I tell is only of a cock,

Who had not run the hazard of his life,
Had he believed his dream, and not his wife:
For women, with a mischief to their kind,
Pervert with bad advice our better mind.
A woman's counsel brought us first to woe,
And made her man his paradise forego,
Where at heart's ease he lived, and might have been
As free from sorrow as he was from sin.
For what the devil had their sex to do,
That, born to folly, they presumed to know,
And could not see the serpent in the grass?
But I myself presume, and let it pass.

    Silence in times of suffering is the best,
'Tis dangerous to disturb a hornet's nest.
In other authors you may find enough,
But all they say of dames is idle stuff.
Legends of lying wits together bound,
The Wife of Bath would throw 'em to the ground;
These are the words of Chanticleer, not mine,
I honour dames, and think their sex divine.

    Now to continue what my tale begun:
Lay Madam Partlet basking in the sun,
Breast-high in sand; her sisters, in a row,
Enjoyed the beams above, the warmth below.
The cock, that of his flesh was ever free,
Sung merrier than the mermaid in the sea;
And so befell, that as he cast his eye
Among the coleworts on a butterfly,
He saw false Reynard where he lay full low;
I need not swear he had no list to crow;
But cried, *Cock, cock*, and gave a sudden start,
As sore dismayed and frighted at his heart.
For birds and beasts, informed by nature, know
Kinds opposite to theirs, and fly their foe.
So Chanticleer, who never saw a fox,
Yet shunned him as a sailor shuns the rocks.

    But the false loon, who could not work his will
By open force, employed his flattering skill:
" I hope, my lord," said he, " I not offend;
Are you afraid of me that am your friend?
I were a beast indeed to do you wrong, '

I, who have loved and honoured you so long :
Stay, gentle sir, nor take a false alarm,
For, on my soul, I never meant you harm !
I come no spy, nor as a traitor press,
To learn the secrets of your soft recess :
Far be from Reynard so profane a thought,
But by the sweetness of your voice was brought :
For, as I bid my beads, by chance I heard
The song as of an angel in the yard ;
A song that would have charmed the infernal
    gods,
And banished horror from the dark abodes :
Had Orpheus sung it in the nether sphere
So much the hymn had pleased the tyrant's ear,
The wife had been detained, to keep the husband
    there.
   My lord your sire familiarly I knew,
A peer deserving such a son as you :
He, with your lady-mother (whom Heaven rest),
Has often graced my house, and been my guest :
To view his living features does me good,
For I am your poor neighbour in the wood ;
And in my cottage should be proud to see
The worthy heir of my friend's family.
   But since I speak of singing, let me say,
As with an upright heart I safely may,
That, save yourself, there breathes not on the ground
One like your father for a silver sound.
So sweetly would he wake the winter day,
That matrons to the church mistook their way,
And thought they heard the merry organ play.
And he to raise his voice with artful care
(What will not beaux attempt to please the fair ?)
On tiptoe stood to sing with greater strength,
And stretched his comely neck at all the length ;
And while he pained his voice to pierce the skies,
As saints in raptures use, would shut his eyes,
That the sound striving through the narrow throat,
His winking might avail to mend the note.
By this, in song he never had his peer,
From sweet Cecilia down to Chanticleer ;

Not Maro's muse, who sung the mighty man,
Nor Pindar's heavenly lyre, nor Horace when a
Your ancestors proceed from race divine :   [swan.
From Brennus and Belinus is your line ;
Who gave to sovereign Rome such loud alarms,
That even the priests were not excused from arms.
    Besides, a famous monk of modern times
Has left of cocks recorded in his rhymes,
That of a parish priest the son and heir
(When sons of priests were from the proverb clear)
Affronted once a cock of noble kind,
And either lamed his legs, or struck him blind ;
For which the clerk his father was disgraced,
And in his benefice another placed.
Now sing, my lord, if not for love of me,
Yet for the sake of sweet Saint Charity ;
Make hills and dales, and earth and heaven rejoice,
And emulate your father's angel-voice."
    The cock was pleased to hear him speak so fair,
And proud beside, as solar people are ;
Nor could the treason from the truth descry,
So was he ravished with this flattery :
So much the more, as from a little elf,
He had a high opinion of himself ;
Though sickly, slender, and not large of limb,
Concluding all the world was made for him.
    Ye princes, raised by poets to the gods,
And Alexandered up in lying odes,
Believe not every flattering knave's report,
There's many a Reynard lurking in the court ;
And he shall be received with more regard,
And listened to, than modest truth is heard.
    This Chanticleer, of whom the story sings,
Stood high upon his toes, and clapped his wings ;
Then stretched his neck, and winked with both his
        eyes,
Ambitious as he sought the Olympic prize.
But while he pained himself to raise his note,
False Reynard rushed, and caught him by the throat.
Then on his back he laid the precious load,
And sought his wonted shelter of the wood ;

Swiftly he made his way, the mischief done,
Of all unheeded, and pursued by none.
  Alas! what stay is there in human state,
Or who can shun inevitable fate?
The doom was written, the decree was past,
Ere the foundations of the world were cast!
In Aries though the sun exalted stood,
His patron-planet to procure his good;
Yet Saturn was his mortal foe, and he,
In Libra raised, opposed the same degree:
The rays both good and bad of equal power,
Each thwarting other, made a mingled hour.
  On Friday morn he dreamt this direful dream,
Cross to the worthy native, in his scheme.
Ah blissful Venus! goddess of delight!
How couldst thou suffer thy devoted knight,
On thy own day, to fall by foe oppressed,
The wight of all the world who served thee best?
Who, true to love, was all for recreation,
And minded not the work of propagation.
Gaufride, who couldst so well in rhyme complain
The death of Richard with an arrow slain,
Why had not I thy Muse, or thou my heart,
To sing this heavy dirge with equal art!
That I like thee on Friday might complain;
For on that day was Cœur de Lion slain.
  No louder cries, when Ilium was in flames,
Were sent to heaven by woeful Trojan dames,
When Pyrrhus tossed on high his burnished blade,
And offered Priam to his father's shade,
Than for the cock the widowed poultry made.
Fair Partlet first, when he was borne from sight,
With sovereign shrieks bewailed her captive knight:
Far louder than the Carthaginian wife,
When Asdrubal her husband lost his life,
When she beheld the smouldering flames ascend,
And all the Punic glories at an end:
Willing into the fires she plunged her head,
With greater ease than others seek their bed.
Not more aghast the matrons of renown,
When tyrant Nero burned the imperial town,

E

Shrieked for the downfall in a doleful cry,
For which their guiltless lords were doomed to die.
  Now to my story I return again :
The trembling widow, and her daughters twain,
This woeful cackling cry with horror heard,
Of those distracted damsels in the yard ;
And starting up, beheld the heavy sight,
How Reynard to the forest took his flight,
And cross his back, as in triumphant scorn,
The hope and pillar of the house was borne.
  " The fox, the wicked fox," was all the cry ;
Out from his house ran every neighbour nigh :
The vicar first, and after him the crew,
With forks and staves the felon to pursue.
Ran Coll our dog, and Talbot with the band,
And Malkin, with her distaff in her hand :
Ran cow and calf, and family of hogs,
In panic horror of pursuing dogs ;
With many a deadly grunt and doleful squeak,
Poor swine, as if their pretty hearts would break.
The shouts of men, the women in dismay,
With shrieks augment the terror of the day.
The ducks, that heard the proclamation cried,
And feared a persecution might betide,
Full twenty mile from town their voyage take,
Obscure in rushes of the liquid lake.
The geese fly o'er the barn ; the bees in arms
Drive headlong from their waxen cells in swarms.
Jack Straw at London-stone with all his rout
Struck not the city with so loud a shout ;
Not when with English hate they did pursue
A Frenchman, or an unbelieving Jew ;
Not when, the welkin rung with one and all ;
And echoes bounded back from Fox's Hall ;
Earth seemed to sink beneath, and heaven above
    to fall.
With might and main they chased the murderous
    fox,
With brazen trumpets, and inflated box,
To kindle Mars with military sounds,
Nor wanted horns to inspire sagacious hounds.

But see how Fortune can confound the wise,
And when they least expect it turn the dice.
The captive cock, who scarce could draw his breath,
And lay within the very jaws of death ;
Yet in his agony his fancy wrought,
And fear supplied him with this happy thought :
" Yours is the prize, victorious prince," said he,
The vicar my defeat and all the village see.
Enjoy your friendly fortune while you may,
And bid the churls that envy you the prey
Call back the mongrel curs, and cease their cry :
See, fools, the shelter of the wood is nigh,
And Chanticleer in your despite shall die ;
He shall be plucked and eaten to the bone."
　" 'Tis well advised, in faith it shall be done ; "
This Reynard said : but as the word he spoke,
The prisoner with a spring from prison broke ;
Then stretched his feathered fans with all his might
And to the neighbouring maple winged his flight.
　Whom, when the traitor safe on tree beheld,
He cursed the gods, with shame and sorrow filled :
Shame for his folly ; sorrow out of time,
For plotting an unprofitable crime :
Yet, mastering both, the artificer of lies
Renews the assault, and his last battery tries.
　" Though I," said he, " did ne'er in thought
　　offend,
How justly may my lord suspect his friend !
The appearance is against me, I confess,
Who seemingly have put you in distress ;
You, if your goodness does not plead my cause,
May think I broke all hospitable laws,
To bear you from your palace-yard by might,
And put your noble person in a fright ;
This, since you take it ill, I must repent,
Though Heaven can witness with no bad intent
I practised it, to make you taste your cheer
With double pleasure, first prepared by fear.
So loyal subjects often seize their prince,
Forced (for his good) to seeming violence,
Yet mean his sacred person not the least offence.

Descend ; so help me Jove as you shall find
That Reynard comes of no dissembling kind."
  " Nay," quoth the cock ; " but I beshrew us both,
If I believe a saint upon his oath :
An honest man may take a knave's advice,
But idiots only may be cozened twice :
Once warned is well bewared ; not flattering lies
Shall soothe me more to sing with winking eyes
And open mouth, for fear of catching flies.
Who blindfold walks upon a river's brim,
When he should see, has he deserved to swim ! "
  " Better, Sir Cock, let all contention cease ;
Come down," said Reynard, " let us treat of peace."
  " A peace with all my soul," said Chanticleer,
" But, with your favour, I will treat it here :
And lest the truce with treason should be mixed,
'Tis my concern to have the tree betwixt."

THE MORAL.

  In this plain fable you the effect may see
Of negligence, and fond credulity :
And learn besides of flatterers to beware,
Then most pernicious when they speak too fair.
The cock and fox, the fool and knave imply ;
The truth is moral, though the tale a lie.
Who spoke in parables, I dare not say ;
But sure he knew it was a pleasing way
Sound sense by plain example to convey.
And in a heathen author we may find,
That pleasure with instruction should be joined ;
So take the corn, and leave the chaff behind.

✳

The Flower and the Leaf; or, The Lady in the Arbour.

A VISION.

Now turning from the wintry signs, the sun
His course exalted through the Ram had run;
And whirling up the skies, his chariot drove
Through Taurus, and the lightsome realms of love,
Where Venus from her orb descends in showers,
To glad the ground and paint the fields with flowers;
When first the tender blades of grass appear,
And buds that yet the blast of Eurus fear
Stand at the door of life, and doubt to clothe the
Till gentle heat and soft repeated rains   [year;
Make the green blood to dance within their veins;
Then, at their call emboldened out they come,
And swell the gems and burst the narrow room;
Broader and broader yet their blooms display,
Salute the welcome sun, and entertain the day.
Then from their breathing souls the sweets repair
To scent the skies, and purge the unwholesome air:
Joy spreads the heart, and with a general song
Spring issues out, and leads the jolly months along.
In that sweet season, as in bed I lay,
And sought in sleep to pass the night away,
I turned my weary side, but still in vain,
Though full of youthful health and void of pain:
Cares I had none to keep me from my rest,
For love had never entered in my breast;
I wanted nothing Fortune could supply,
Nor did she slumber till that hour deny.

I wondered then, but after found it true,
Much joy had dried away the balmy dew :
Seas would be pools without the brushing air
To curl the waves ; and sure some little care
Should weary nature so, to make her want repair.
　　When chanticleer the second watch had sung,
Scorning the scorner sleep, from bed I sprung ;
And dressing, by the moon, in loose array
Passed out in open air, preventing day,
And sought a goodly grove, as fancy led my way.
Straight as a line in beauteous order stood
Of oaks unshorn a venerable wood ;
Fresh was the grass beneath, and every tree,
At distance planted in a due degree,
Their branching arms in air with equal space
Stretched to their neighbours with a long embrace ;
And the new leaves on every bough were seen,
Some ruddy-coloured, some of lighter green.
The painted birds, companions of the spring,
Hopping from spray to spray, were heard to sing.
Both eyes and ears received a like delight,
Enchanting music, and a charming sight.
On Philomel I fixed my whole desire,
And listened for the queen of all the choir :
Fain would I hear her heavenly voice to sing ;
And wanted yet an omen to the spring.
　　Attending long in vain, I took the way
Which through a path but scarcely printed lay ;
In narrow mazes oft it seemed to meet,
And looked as lightly pressed by fairy feet.
Wandering I walked alone, for still methought
To some strange end so strange a path was wrought :
At last it led me where an arbour stood,
The sacred receptacle of the wood :
This place unmarked, though oft I walked the
　　　green,
In all my progress I had never seen ;
And seized at once with wonder and delight,
Gazed all around me, new to the transporting sight.
'Twas benched with turf, and, goodly to be seen,
The thick young grass arose in fresher green,

The mound was newly made, no sight could pass
Betwixt the nice partitions of the grass,
The well-united sods so closely lay;
And all around the shades defended it from day;
For sycamores with eglantine were spread,
A hedge about the sides, a covering overhead.
And so the fragrant brier was wove between,
The sycamore and flowers were mixed with green,
That nature seemed to vary the delight,
And satisfied at once the smell and sight.
The master-workman of the bower was known
Through fairy-lands, and built for Oberon;
Who twining leaves with such proportion drew,
They rose by measure, and by rule they grew;
No mortal tongue can half the beauty tell,
For none but hands divine could work so well.
Both roof and sides were like a parlour made,
A soft recess, and a cool summer shade;
The hedge was set so thick, no foreign eye
The persons placed within it could espy;
But all that passed without with ease was seen,
As if nor fence nor tree was placed between.
'Twas bordered with a field; and some was plain
With grass, and some was sowed with rising grain.
That, now the dew with spangles decked the ground,
A sweeter spot of earth was never found.
I looked and looked, and still with new delight;
Such joy my soul, such pleasures filled my sight:
And the fresh eglantine exhaled a breath
Whose odours were of power to raise from death.
Nor sullen discontent nor anxious care,
Even though brought thither, could inhabit there:
But thence they fled as from their mortal foe;
For this sweet place could only pleasure know.
    Thus as I mused, I cast aside my eye,
And saw a medlar-tree was planted nigh.
The spreading branches made a goodly show,
And full of opening blooms was every bough:
A goldfinch there I saw with gaudy pride
Of painted plumes, that hopped from side to
    side,

Still pecking as she passed ; and still she drew
The sweets from every flower, and sucked the
    dew :
Sufficed at length, she warbled in her throat,
And tuned her voice to many a merry note,
But indistinct, and neither sweet nor clear,
Yet such as soothed my soul, and pleased my ear.
   Her short performance was no sooner tried,
When she I sought, the nightingale, replied :
So sweet, so shrill, so variously she sung,
That the grove echoed, and the valleys rung,
And I so ravished with her heavenly note,
I stood entranced, and had no room for thought,
But all o'erpowered with ecstacy of bliss,
Was in a pleasing dream of Paradise :
At length I waked, and looking round the bower,
Searched every tree, and pried on every flower,
If anywhere by chance I might espy
The rural poet of the melody ;
For still methought she sung not far away :
At last I found her on a laurel spray.
Close by my side she sat, and fair in sight,
Full in a line, against her opposite,
Where stood with eglantine the laurel twined ;
And both their native sweets were well conjoined.
   On the green bank I sat, and listened long
(Sitting was more convenient for the song) ;
Nor till her lay was ended could I move,
But wished to dwell for ever in the grove.
Only methought the time too swiftly passed,
And every note I feared would be the last.
My sight and smell and hearing were employed,
And all three senses in full gust enjoyed.
And what alone did all the rest surpass,
The sweet possession of the fairy place ;
Single, and conscious to myself alone
Of pleasures to the excluded world unknown ;
Pleasures which nowhere else were to be found,
And all Elysium in a spot of ground.
   Thus while I sat intent to see and hear,
And drew perfumes of more than vital air,

All suddenly I heard the approaching sound
Of vocal music on the enchanted ground ;
An host of saints it seemed, so full the choir,
As if the blessed above did all conspire
To join their voices, and neglect the lyre.
At length there issued from the grove behind
A fair assembly of the female kind :
A train less fair, as ancient fathers tell,
Seduced the sons of heaven to rebel.
I pass their form, and every charming grace ;
Less than an angel would their worth debase :
But their attire, like liveries of a kind
All rich and rare, is fresh within my mind.
In velvet white as snow the troop was gowned,
The seams with sparkling emeralds set around :
Their hoods and sleeves the same ; and purfled o'er
With diamonds, pearls, and all the shining store
Of Eastern pomp : their long descending train,
With rubies edged and sapphires, swept the plain :
High on their heads, with jewels richly set,
Each lady wore a radiant coronet.
Beneath the circles, all the choir was graced
With chaplets green on their fair foreheads placed,
Of laurel some, of woodbine many more ;
And wreaths of *Agnus castus* others bore :
These last, who with those virgin crowns were
Appeared in higher honour than the rest.   [dressed,
They danced around : but in the midst was seen
A lady of a more majestic mien ;
By stature and by beauty marked their sovereign
  queen.
 She in the midst began with sober grace ;
Her servants' eyes were fixed upon her face,
And as she moved or turned, her motions viewed,
Her measures kept, and step by step pursued.
Methought she trod the ground with greater grace,
With more of godhead shining in her face ;
And as in beauty she surpassed the choir,
So nobler than the rest was her attire.
A crown of ruddy gold enclosed her brow,
Plain without pomp, and rich without a show :

A branch of *Agnus castus* in her hand
She bore aloft (her sceptre of command);
Admired, adored by all the circling crowd,
For wheresoe'er she turned her face, they bowed:
And as she danced, a roundelay she sung,
In honour of the Laurel, ever young:
She raised her voice on high, and sung so clear,
The fawns came scudding from the groves to hear:
And all the bending forest lent an ear.
At every close she made, the attending throng
Replied, and bore the burden of the song:
So just, so small, yet in so sweet a note,
It seemed the music melted in the throat.

Thus dancing on, and singing as they danced,
They to the middle of the mead advanced,
Till round my arbour a new ring they made,
And footed it about the secret shade.
O'erjoyed to see the jolly troop so near,
But somewhat awed, I shook with holy fear;
Yet not so much, but that I noted well
Who did the most in song or dance excel.

Not long I had observed, when from afar
I heard a sudden symphony of war;
The neighing coursers, and the soldiers' cry,
And sounding trumps that seemed to tear the sky.
I saw soon after this, behind the grove
From whence the ladies did in order move,
Come issuing out in arms a warrior-train,
That like a deluge poured upon the plain:
On barbéd steeds they rode in proud array,
Thick as the college of the bees in May,
When swarming o'er the dusky fields they fly,
New to the flowers, and intercept the sky.
So fierce they drove, their coursers were so fleet,
That the turf trembled underneath their feet.

To tell their costly furniture were long,
The summer's day would end before the song:
To purchase but the tenth of all their store
Would make the mighty Persian monarch poor.
Yet what I can, I will; before the rest
The trumpets issued, in white mantles dressed;

A numerous group, and all their heads around
With chaplets green of cerrial-oak were crowned,
And at each trumpet was a banner bound
Which waving in the wind displayed at large
Their master's coat of arms, and knightly charge.
Broad were the banners, and of snowy hue,
A purer web the silkworm never drew.
The chief about their necks the scutcheons wore,
With orient pearls and jewels powdered o'er :
Broad were their collars too, and every one
Was set about with many a costly stone.
Next these, of kings at arms a goodly train
In proud array came prancing o'er the plain :
Their cloaks were cloth of silver mixed with
    gold,
And garlands green around their temples rolled :
Rich crowns were on their royal scutcheons placed,
With sapphires, diamonds, and with rubies graced :
And as the trumpets their appearance made,
So these in habits were alike arrayed ;
But with a pace more sober, and more slow,
And twenty, rank in rank, they rode a-row.
The pursuivants came next, in number more ;
And like the heralds each his scutcheon bore :
Clad in white velvet all their troop they led,
With each an open chaplet on his head.
    Nine royal knights in equal rank succeed,
Each warrior mounted on a fiery steed,
In golden armour glorious to behold ;
The rivets of their arms were nailed with gold.
Their surcoats of white ermine-fur were made,
With cloth of gold between, that cast a glittering
    shade ;
The trappings of their steeds were of the same ;
The golden fringe even set the ground on flame,
And drew a precious trail : a crown divine
Of Laurel did about their temples twine.
    Three henchmen were for every knight assigned,
All in rich livery clad, and of a kind ;
White velvet, but unshorn, for cloaks they wore,
And each within his hand a truncheon bore :

The foremost held a helm of rare device ;
A prince's ransom would not pay the price.
The second bore the buckler of his knight,
The third of cornel-wood a spear upright,
Headed with piercing steel, and polished bright.
Like to their lords their equipage was seen,
And all their foreheads crowned with garlands green.
　　And after these came, armed with spear and shield,
An host so great as covered all the field :
And all their foreheads, like the knights before,
With laurels ever green were shaded o'er,
Or oak, or other leaves of lasting kind,
Tenacious of the stem and firm against the wind.
Some in their hands, besides the lance and shield,
The boughs of woodbine or of hawthorn held,
Or branches for their mystic emblems took,
Of palm, of laurel, or of cerrial-oak.
　　Thus marching to the trumpet's lofty sound,
Drawn in two lines adverse they wheeled around,
And in the middle meadow took their ground.
Among themselves the tourney they divide,
In equal squadrons ranged on either side.
Then turned their horses' heads, and man to man
And steed to steed opposed, the jousts began.
They lightly set their lances in the rest,
And, at the sign, against each other pressed :
They met ; I sitting at my ease beheld
The mixed events and fortunes of the field.　[man,
Some broke their spears, some tumbled horse and
And round the fields the lightened coursers ran.
An hour and more, like tides in equal sway,
They rushed, and won by turns and lost the day :
At length the nine who still together held
Their fainting foes to shameful flight compelled,
And with resistless force o'erran the field.
Thus, to their fame, when finished was the fight,
The victors from their lofty steeds alight :
Like them dismounted all the warlike train,
And two by two proceeded o'er the plain :
Till to the fair assembly they advanced,
Who near the secret arbour sung and danced.

The ladies left their measures at the sight,
To meet the chiefs returning from the fight,
And each with open arms embraced her chosen
Amid the plain a spreading Laurel stood, [knight,
The grace and ornament of all the wood :
That pleasing shade they sought, a soft retreat
From sudden April showers, a shelter from the heat :
Her leavy arms with such extent were spread,
So near the clouds was her aspiring head,
That hosts of birds that wing the liquid air,
Perched in the boughs, had nightly lodging there :
And flocks of sheep beneath the shade from far
Might hear the rattling hail and wintry war,
From heaven's inclemency here found retreat,
Enjoyed the cool, and shunned the scorching heat.
A hundred knights might there at ease abide.
And every knight a lady by his side.
The trunk itself such odours did bequeath, [breath.
That a Moluccan breeze to these was common
The lords and ladies here, approaching, paid
Their homage, with a low obeisance made,
And seemed to venerate the sacred shade.
These rites performed, their pleasures they pursue,
With song of love, and mix with measures new ;
Around the holy tree their dance they frame,
And every champion leads his chosen dame.
   I cast my sight upon the farther field,
And a fresh object of delight beheld :
For from the region of the west I heard
New music sound, and a new troop appeared
Of knights and ladies mixed, a jolly band,
But all on foot they marched, and hand in hand.
   The ladies dressed in rich symarrs were seen
Of Florence satin, flowered with white and green,
And for a shade betwixt the bloomy gridelin.
The borders of their petticoats below
Were guarded thick with rubies on a-row ;
And every damsel wore upon her head
Of Flowers a garland blended white and red.
Attire I in mantles all the knights were seen,
That gratified the view with cheerful green ;

Their chaplets of their ladies' colours were,
Composed of white and red, to shade their shining
Before the merry troop the minstrels played ; [hair.
.All in their masters' liveries were arrayed,
And clad in green, and on their temples wore
The chaplets white and red their ladies bore.
Their instruments were various in their kind,
Some for the bow, and some for breathing wind ;
The sawtry, pipe, and hautbois' noisy band,
And the soft lute trembling beneath the touching
A tuft of daisies on a flowery lea   [hand.
They saw, and thitherward they bent their way ;
To this both knights and dames their homage made,
And due obeisance to the daisy paid.
And then the band of flutes began to play,
To which a lady sung a virelay :
And still at every close she would repeat
The burden of the song, *The daisy is so sweet.*
The daisy is so sweet, when she begun,
The troop of knights and dames continued on.
The concert and the voice so charmed my ear,
And soothed my soul, that it was heaven to hear.
   But soon their pleasure passed : at noon of day
The sun with sultry beams began to play :
Not Sirius shoots a fiercer flame from high,
When with his poisonous breath he blasts the sky :
Then drooped the fading flowers, their beauty fled,
And closed their sickly eyes, and hung the head,
And rivelled up with heat, lay dying in their bed.
The ladies gasped, and scarcely could respire ;
The breath they drew, no longer air but fire ;
The fainty knights were scorched, and knew not
To run for shelter, for no shade was near.   [where
And after this the gathering clouds amain
Poured down a storm of rattling hail and rain ;
And lightning flashed betwixt ; the field and flowers,
Burnt up before, were buried in the showers.
The ladies and the knights, no shelter nigh,
Bare to the weather and the wintry sky,
Were dropping wet, disconsolate, and wan,
And through their thin array received the rain ;

While those in white, protected by the tree, [free;
Saw pass the vain assault, and stood from danger
But as compassion moved their gentle minds,
When ceased the storm, and silent were the winds,
Displeased at what, not suffering, they had seen,
They went to cheer the faction of the green :
The queen in white array, before her band,
Saluting, took her rival by the hand ;
So did the knights and dames, with courtly grace,
And with behaviour sweet their foes embrace.
Then thus the queen with Laurel on her brow :
" Fair sister, I have suffered in your woe ;
Nor shall be wanting aught within my power
For your relief in my refreshing bower."
That other answered with a lowly look,
And soon the gracious invitation took :
For ill at ease both she and all her train
The scorching sun had borne, and beating rain.
Like courtesy was used by all in white,
Each dame a dame received, and every knight a
    knight.
The laurel champions with their swords invade
The neighbouring forests, where the jousts were
    made,
And serewood from the rotten hedges took,
And seeds of latent fire from flints provoke :
A cheerful blaze arose, and by the fire
They warmed their frozen feet, and dried their wet
    attire.
Refreshed with heat, the ladies sought around
For virtuous herbs, which gathered from the ground,
They squeezed the juice, and cooling ointment made,
Which on their sunburnt cheeks and their chapt
    skins they laid ;
Then sought green salads, which they bade them eat,
A sovereign remedy for inward heat.
    The Lady of the Leaf ordained a feast,
And made the Lady of the Flower her guest :
When lo ! a bower ascended on the plain,
With sudden seats ordained, and large for either
    train.

This bower was near my pleasant arbour placed,
That I could hear and see whatever passed :
The ladies sat with each a knight between,
Distinguished by their colours white and green ;
The vanquished party with the victors joined,
Nor wanted sweet discourse, the banquet of the
    mind.
Meantime the minstrels played on either side,
Vain of their art, and for the mastery vied :
The sweet contention lasted for an hour,
And reached my secret arbour from the bower.

The sun was set ; and Vesper, to supply
His absent beams, had lighted up the sky ;
When Philomel, officious all the day
To sing the service of the ensuing May,
Fled from her laurel shade, and winged her flight
Directly to the queen arrayed in white ;
And hopping sat familiar on her hand,
A new musician, and increased the band.

The goldfinch, who, to shun the scalding heat,
Had changed the medlar for a safer seat,
And hid in bushes scaped the bitter shower,
Now perched upon the Lady of the Flower ;
And either songster holding out their throats,
And folding up their wings, renewed their notes ;
As if all day, preluding to the fight,
They only had rehearsed, to sing by night.
The banquet ended, and the battle done,
They danced by starlight and the friendly moon :
And when they were to part, the laureat queen
Supplied with steeds the Lady of the Green,
Her and her train conducting on the way
The moon to follow, and avoid the day.

This when I saw, inquisitive to know
The secret moral of the mystic show,
I started from my shade, in hopes to find
Some nymph to satisfy my longing mind ;
And as my fair adventure fell, I found
A lady all in white with laurel crowned,
Who closed the rear and softly paced along,
Repeating to herself the former song.

With due respect my body I inclined,
As to some being of superior kind,
And made my court according to the day,
Wishing her queen and her a happy May.
" Great thanks, my daughter," with a gracious bow,
She said ; and I, who much desired to know
Of whence she was, yet fearful how to break
My mind, adventured humbly thus to speak :
" Madam, might I presume and not offend,
So may the stars and shining moon attend
Your nightly sports, as you vouchsafe to tell,
What nymphs they were who mortal forms excel,
And what the knights who fought in listed fields
    so well ? "
   To this the dame replied : " Fair daughter, know,
That what you saw was all a fairy show ;
And all those airy shapes you now behold
Were human bodies once, and clothed with earthly
    mould.
Our souls, not yet prepared for upper light,
Till doomsday wander in the shades of night ;
This only holiday of all the year,
We privileged in sunshine may appear :
With songs and dance we celebrate the day,
And with due honours usher in the May.
At other times we reign by night alone,
And posting through the skies pursue the moon ;
But when the morn arises, none are found,
For cruel Demogorgon walks the round,
And if he finds a fairy lag in light,
He drives the wretch before, and lashes into night.
   All courteous are by kind ; and ever proud
With friendly offices to help the good.
In every land we have a larger space
Than what is known to you of mortal race ;
Where we with green adorn our fairy bowers,
And even this grove, unseen before, is ours.
Know further, every lady clothed in white,
And crowned with oak and laurel every knight,
Are servants to the Leaf, by liveries known
Of innocence ; and I myself am one.

Saw you not her so graceful to behold,
In white attire, and crowned with radiant gold?
The sovereign lady of our land is she,
Diana called, the queen of chastity;
And, for the spotless name of maid she bears,
That *Agnus castus* in her hand appears;
And all her train, with leafy chaplets crowned,
Were for unblamed virginity renowned;
But those the chief and highest in command
Who bear those holy branches in their hand.
The knights adorned with laurel crowns are they
Whom death nor danger ever could dismay,
Victorious names, who made the world obey;
Who, while they lived, in deeds of arms excelled,
And after death for deities were held.
But those who wear the woodbine on their brow
Were knights of love, who never broke their vow;
Firm to their plighted faith, and ever free
From fears and fickle chance and jealousy.
The lords and ladies, who the woodbine bear,
As true as Tristram and Isolda were."
    "But what are those," said I, "the unconquered
       nine,
Who, crowned with laurel-wreaths, in golden
       armour shine?
And who the knights in green, and what the train
Of ladies dressed with daisies on the plain?
Why both the bands in worship disagree,
And some adore the flower, and some the tree?"
    "Just is your suit, fair daughter," said the dame;
"Those laurelled chiefs were men of mighty fame;
Nine Worthies were they called of different rites,
Three Jews, three Pagans, and three Christian
       knights.
These, as you see, ride foremost in the field,
As they the foremost rank of honour held,
And all in deeds of chivalry excelled:
Their temples wreathed with leaves that still renew,
For deathless laurel is the victor's due.
Who bear the bows were knights in Arthur's reign,
Twelve they, and twelve the peers of Charlemain:

For bows the strength of brawny arms imply
Emblems of valour and of victory.
Behold an order yet of newer date,
Doubling their number, equal in their state;
Our England's ornament, the crown's defence,
In battle brave, protectors of their prince:
Unchanged by fortune, to their sovereign true,
For which their manly legs are bound with blue.
These, of the Garter called, of faith unstained,
In fighting fields the laurel have obtained,
And well repaid those honours which they gained.
The laurel wreaths were first by Cæsar worn,
And still they Cæsar's successors adorn;
One Leaf of this is immortality,
And more of worth than all the world can buy."
    "One doubt remains," said I : "the dames in
        green,
What were their qualities, and who their queen?"
"Flora commands," said she, "those nymphs and
        knights
Who lived in slothful ease and loose delights;
Who never acts of honour durst pursue,
The men inglorious knights, the ladies all untrue;
Who, nursed in idleness, and trained in courts,
Passed all their precious hours in plays and sports,
Till death behind came stalking on unseen,
And withered, like the storm, the freshness of their
        green.
These, and their mates, enjoy their present hour,
And therefore pay their homage to the Flower.
But knights in knightly deeds should persevere,
And still continue what at first they were;
Continue, and proceed in honour's fair career.
No room for cowardice, or dull delay;
From good to better they should urge their way.
For this with golden spurs the chiefs are graced,
With pointed rowels armed to mend their haste;
For this with lasting Leaves their brows are bound,
For Laurel is the sign of labour crowned,
Which bears the bitter blast, nor shaken falls to
        ground:

From winter winds it suffers no decay,
For ever fresh and fair, and every month is May.
Even when the vital sap retreats below,
Even when the hoary head is hid in snow,
The life is in the Leaf, and still between
The fits of falling snow appears the streaky green.
Not so the Flower, which lasts for little space,
A short-lived good, and an uncertain grace ;
This way and that the feeble stem is driven,
Weak to sustain the storms and injuries of heaven.
Propped by the spring, it lifts aloft the head,
But of a sickly beauty, soon to shed ;
In summer living, and in winter dead.
For things of tender kind, for pleasure made,
Shoot up with swift increase, and sudden are
        decayed."
    With humble words, the wisest I could frame,
And proffered service, I repaid the dame ;
That of her grace she gave her maid to know
The secret meaning of this moral show.
And she, to prove what profit I had made
Of mystic truth, in fables first conveyed,
Demanded till the next returning May,
Whether the Leaf or Flower I would obey ?
I chose the Leaf ; she smiled with sober cheer,
And wished me fair adventure for the year,
And gave me charms and sigils, for defence
Against ill tongues that scandal innocence :
" But I," said she, " my fellows must pursue,
Already past the plain, and out of view."
    We parted thus ; I homeward sped my way,
Bewildered in the wood till-dawn of day :
And met the merry crew who danced about the May.
Then late refreshed with sleep, I rose to write
The visionary vigils of the night.
Blush, as thou mayest, my little book, for shame,
Nor hope with homely verse to purchase fame ;
For such thy maker chose ; and so designed
Thy simple style to suit thy lowly kind.

In days of old, when Arthur filled the throne,
Whose acts and fame to foreign lands were blown,
The King of Elves and little Fairy Queen
Gambolled on heaths, and danced on every green ;
And where the jolly troop had led the round,
The grass unbidden rose, and marked the ground.
Nor darkling did they dance ; the silver light
Of Phœbe served to guide their steps aright,
And, with their tripping pleased, prolonged the night.
Her beams they followed, where at full she played,
Nor longer than she shed her horns they stayed,
From thence with airy flight to foreign lands con-
Above the rest our Britain held they dear,   [veyed.
More solemnly they kept their sabbaths here,
And made more spacious rings, and revelled half
      the year.
   I speak of ancient times ; for now the swain
Returning late may pass the woods in vain,
And never hope to see the nightly train ;
In vain the dairy now with mints is dressed,
The dairy-maid expects no fairy guest
To skim the bowls and after pay the feast.
She sighs, and shakes her empty shoes in vain,
No silver penny to reward her pain :
For priests with prayers, and other godly gear,
Have made the merry goblins disappear ;
And where they played their merry pranks before,
Have sprinkled holy water on the floor ;
And friars that through the wealthy regions run,
Thick as the motes that twinkle in the sun,

Resort to farmers rich, and bless their halls,
And exorcise the beds, and cross the walls :
This makes the fairy quires forsake the place,
When once 'tis hallowed with the rites of grace :
But in the walks, where wicked elves have been,
The learning of the parish now is seen ;
The midnight parson posting o'er the green
With gown tucked up to wakes, for Sunday next
With humming ale encouraging his text ;
Nor wants the holy leer to country-girl betwixt.
From fiends and imps he sets the village free,
There haunts not any incubus but he.
The maids and women need no danger fear
To walk by night, and sanctity so near ;
For by some haycock, or some shady thorn,
He bids his beads both evensong and morn.
. It so befell in this King Arthur's reign,
A lusty knight was pricking o'er the plain ;
A bachelor he was, and of the courtly train.
.It happened as he rode, a damsel gay
In russet robes to market took her way ;
Soon on the girl he cast an amorous eye,
So straight she walked, and on her pasterns high :
If seeing her behind he liked her pace,
Now turning short he better liked her face.
He lights in haste, and, full of youthful fire,
By force accomplished his obscene desire.
This done, away he rode, not unespied,
For swarming at his back the country cried :
And once in view they never lost the sight,
But seized, and pinioned brought to court the knight.
    Then courts of kings were held in high renown,
Ere made the common brothels of the town ;
There virgins honourable vows received,
But chaste as maids in monasteries lived :
The King himself, to nuptial ties a slave,
No bad example to his poets gave ;
And they, not bad, but in a vicious age,
Had not to please the prince debauched the stage.
    Now what should Arthur do? He loved the knight,
But sovereign monarchs are the source of right :

Moved by the damsel's tears and common cry,
He doomed the brutal ravisher to die.
But fair Geneura rose in his defence,
And prayed so hard for mercy from the prince,
That to his Queen the King the offender gave,
And left it in her power to kill or save.
This gracious act the ladies all approve,
Who thought it much a man should die for love ;
And with their mistress joined in close debate
(Covering their kindness with dissembled hate),
If not to free him, to prolong his fate.
At last agreed, they call him by consent
Before the Queen and female parliament ;
And the fair speaker, rising from the chair,
Did thus the judgment of the house declare.
  " Sir knight, though I have asked thy life, yet still
Thy destiny depends upon my will :
Nor hast thou other surety than the grace
Not due to thee from our offended race.
But as our kind is of a softer mould,
And cannot blood without a sigh behold,
I grant thee life ; reserving still the power
To take the forfeit when I see my hour ;
Unless thy answer to my next demand
Shall set thee free from our avenging hand.
The question, whose solution I require,
Is what the sex of women most desire ?
In this dispute thy judges are at strife ;
Beware, for on thy wit depends thy life.
Yet (lest, surprised, unknowing what to say,
Thou damn thyself) we give thee farther day ;
A year is thine to wander at thy will ;
And learn from others, if thou wantst the skill.
But not to hold our proffered turn in scorn,
Good sureties will we have for thy return,
That at the time prefixed thou shalt obey,
And at thy pledge's peril keep thy day."
  Woe was the knight at this severe command,
But well he knew 'twas bootless to withstand.
The terms accepted, as the fair ordain,
He put in bail for his return again ;

And promised answer at the day assigned,
The best with Heaven's assistance he could find.
  His leave thus taken, on his way he went
With heavy heart, and full of discontent,
Misdoubting much, and fearful of the event.
'Twas hard the truth of such a point to find,
As was not yet agreed among the kind.
Thus on he went; still anxious more and more,
Asked all he met, and knocked at every door;
Inquired of men; but made his chief request
To learn from women what they loved the best.
They answered each according to her mind,
To please herself, not all the female kind.
One was for wealth, another was for place;
Crones old and ugly wished a better face;
The widow's wish was oftentimes to wed;
The wanton maids were all for sport a-bed;
Some said the sex were pleased with handsome lies,
And some gross flattery loved without disguise.
" Truth is," says one, " he seldom fails to win
Who flatters well; for that's our darling sin.
But long attendance, and a duteous mind,
Will work even with the wisest of the kind."
One thought the sex's prime felicity
Was from the bonds of wedlock to be free;
Their pleasures, hours, and actions all their own,
And uncontrolled to give account to none.
Some wish a husband-fool; but such are curst,
For fools perverse of husbands are the worst:
All women would be counted chaste and wise,
Nor should our spouses see but with our eyes;
For fools will prate; and though they want the wit
To find close faults, yet open blots will hit;
Though better for their ease to hold their tongue,
For womankind was never in the wrong.
So noise ensues, and quarrels last for life;
The wife abhors the fool, the fool the wife.
And some men say, that great delight have we
To be for truth extolled, and secrecy:
And constant in one purpose still to dwell,
And not our husband's counsels to reveal.

But that's a fable : for our sex is frail,
Inventing rather than not tell a tale.
Like leaky sieves, no secrets we can hold ;
Witness the famous tale that Ovid told.
    Midas the king, as in his book appears,
By Phœbus was endowed with ass's ears,
Which under his long locks he well concealed,
As monarch's vices must not be revealed,
For fear the people have 'em in the wind,
Who long ago were neither dumb nor blind ;
Nor apt to think from heaven their title
    springs,
Since Jove and Mars left off begetting kings.
This Midas knew ; and durst communicate
To none but to his wife his ears of state ;
One must be trusted, and he thought her fit,
As passing prudent, and a parlous wit.
To this sagacious confessor he went,
And told her what a gift the gods had sent ;
But told it under matrimonial seal,
With strict injunction never to reveal.
The secret heard, she plighted him her troth
(And sacred sure is every woman's oath)
The royal malady should rest unknown,
Both for her husband's honour and her own ;
But ne'ertheless she pined with discontent ;
The counsel rumbled till it found a vent.
The thing she knew she was obliged to hide ;
By interest and by oath the wife was tied,
But if she told it not, the woman died.
Loth to betray a husband and a prince,
But she must burst, or blab ; and no pretence
Of honour tied her tongue from self-defence.
A marshy ground commodiously was near,
Thither she ran, and held her breath for fear,
Lest if a word she spoke of any thing,
That word might be the secret of the king.
Thus full of counsel to the fen she went,
Griped all the way, and longing for a vent ;
Arrived, by pure necessity compelled,
On her majestic marrow-bones she kneeled ;

Then to the water's brink she laid her head,
And as a bittour bumps within a reed,
" To thee alone, O lake," she said, " I tell
(And, as thy queen, command thee to conceal),
Beneath his locks, the king, my husband, wears
A goodly royal pair of ass's ears :
Now I have eased my bosom of the pain,
Till the next longing fit return again."
    Thus through a woman was the secret known ;
Tell us, and in effect you tell the town.
But to my tale. The knight with heavy cheer,
Wandering in vain, had now consumed the
        year ;
One day was only left to solve the doubt,
Yet knew no more than when he first set out.
But home he must, and as the award had been,
Yield up his body captive to the Queen.
In this despairing state he happed to ride,
As fortune led him, by a forest side ;
Lonely the vale, and full of horror stood,
Brown with the shade of a religious wood :
When full before him at the noon of night
(The moon was up, and shot a gleamy light),
He saw a quire of ladies in a round
That featly footing seemed to skim the ground ;
Thus dancing hand in hand, so light they were,
He knew not where they trod, on earth or air.
At speed he drove, and came a sudden guest,
In hope where many women were, at least
Some one by chance might answer his request.
But faster than his horse the ladies flew,
And in a trice were vanished out of view.
    One only hag remained : but fouler far
Than grandame apes in Indian forests are :
Against a withered oak she leaned her weight,
Propped on her trusty staff, not half upright,
And dropped an awkward courtesy to the knight.
Then said, "What make you, sir, so late abroad
Without a guide, and this no beaten road ?
Or want you aught that here you hope to find,
Or travel for some trouble in your mind ?

The last I guess; and if I read aright,
Those of our sex are bound to serve a knight.
Perhaps good counsel may your grief assuage,
Then tell your pain, for wisdom is in age."
  To this the knight: "Good mother, would you
The secret cause and spring of all my woe? [know
My life must with to-morrow's light expire,
Unless I tell what women most desire.
Now could you help me at this hard essay,
Or for your inborn goodness or for pay,
Yours is my life, redeemed by your advice,
Ask what you please, and I will pay the price:
The proudest kerchief of the court shall rest
Well satisfied of what they love the best."
" Plight me thy faith," quoth she, "that what I ask,
Thy danger over, and performed the task,
That thou shalt give for hire of thy demand;
Here take thy oath, and seal it on my hand;
I warrant thee, on peril of my life,
Thy words shall please both widow, maid, and wife."
  More words there needed not to move the knight,
To take her offer, and his truth to plight.
With that she spread her mantle on the ground,
And, first inquiring whither he was bound,
Bade him not fear, though long and rough the way,
At court he should arrive ere break of day:
His horse should find the way without a guide.
She said: with fury they began to ride,
He on the midst, the beldam at his side.
The horse, what devil drove I cannot tell,
But only this, they sped their journey well;
And all the way the crone informed the knight,
How he should answer the demand aright.
  To court they came; the news was quickly spread
Of his returning to redeem his head.
The female senate was assembled soon,
With all the mob of women in the town:
The Queen sat lord chief-justice of the hall,
And bade the crier cite the criminal.
The knight appeared; and silence they proclaim:
Then first the culprit answered to his name;

And, after forms of laws, was last required
To name the thing that women most desired.
The offender, taught his lesson by the way,
And by his counsel ordered what to say,
Thus bold began : " My lady liege," said he,
" What all your sex desire is *Sovereignty*.
The wife affects her husband to command ;
All must be hers, both money, house, and land :
The maids are mistresses even in their name,
And of their servants full dominion claim.
This, at the peril of my head, I say,
A blunt plain truth, the sex aspires to sway,
You to rule all, while we, like slaves, obey."

    There was not one, or widow, maid, or wife,
But said the knight had well deserved his life.
Even fair Geneura with a blush confessed
The man had found what women love the best.

    Up starts the beldam, who was there unseen,
And reverence made, accosted thus the Queen :
" My liege," said she, " before the court arise,
May I, poor wretch, find favour in your eyes,
To grant my just request : 'twas I who taught
The knight this answer, and inspired his thought.
None but a woman could a man direct
To tell us women what we most affect.
But first I swore him on his knightly troth
(And here demand performance of his oath),
To grant the boon that next I should desire ;
He gave his faith, and I expect my hire :
My promise is fulfilled : I saved his life,
And claim his debt, to take me for his wife."
The knight was asked, nor could his oath deny,
But hoped they would not force him to comply.
The women, who would rather wrest the laws
Than let a sister-plaintiff lose the cause
(As judges on the bench more gracious are,
And more attent to brothers of the bar),
Cried, one and all, the suppliant should have right,
And to the grandame hag adjudged the knight.

    In vain he sighed, and oft with tears desired
Some reasonable suit might be required.

But still the crone was constant to her note ;
The more he spoke, the more she stretched her
In vain he proffered all his goods, to save   [throat.
His body destined to that living grave.
The liquorish hag rejects the pelf with scorn,
And nothing but the man would serve her turn.
" Not all the wealth of Eastern kings," said she,
" Have power to part my plighted love and me ;
And, old and ugly as I am, and poor,
Yet never will I break the faith I swore ;
For mine thou art by promise, during life,
And I thy loving and obedient wife."

     " My love I nay, rather my damnation thou,"
Said he : " nor am I bound to keep my vow ;
The fiend, thy sire, has sent thee from below,
Else how couldst thou my secret sorrows know ?
Avaunt, old witch ! for I renounce thy bed :
The Queen may take the forfeit of my head
Ere any of my race so foul a crone shall wed."

     Both heard, the judge pronounced against the
          knight ;
So was he married in his own despite :
And all day after hid him as an owl,
Not able to sustain a sight so foul.
Perhaps the reader thinks I do him wrong,
To pass the marriage feast and nuptial song :
Mirth there was none, the man was *à-la-mort*,
And little courage had to make his court.
To bed they went, the bridegroom and the bride :
Was never such an ill-paired couple tied :
Restless he tossed, and tumbled to and fro,
And rolled, and wriggled farther off for woe.
The good old wife lay smiling by his side,
And caught him in her quivering arms, and cried,
" When you my ravished predecessor saw,
You were not then become this man of straw ;
Had you been such you might have scaped the law.
Is this the custom of King Arthur's court ?
Are all Round-Table Knights of such a sort ?
Remember I am she who saved your life,
Your loving, lawful, and complying wife :

Nor thus you swore in your unhappy hour,
Nor I for this return employed my power.
In time of need I was your faithful friend;
Nor did I since, nor ever will offend.
Believe me, my loved lord, 'tis much unkind;
What fury has possessed your altered mind?
Thus on my wedding night—without pretence—
Come, turn this way, or tell me my offence.
If not your wife, let reason's rule persuade,
Name but my fault, amends shall soon be made."

 "Amends! nay, that's impossible," said he,
"What change of age, or ugliness, can be?
Or could Medea's magic mend thy face,
Thou art descended from so mean a race,
That never knight was matched with such disgrace.
What wonder, madam, if I move my side,
When, if I turn, I turn to such a bride?"

 "And is this all that troubles you so sore?"
"And what the devil couldst thou wish me more?"
"Ah, benedicite!" replied the crone:
"Then cause of just complaining have you none.
The remedy to this were soon applied,
Would you be like the bridegroom to the bride:
But, for you say a long descended race,
And wealth, and dignity, and power, and place,
Make gentlemen, and that your high degree
Is much disparaged to be matched with me;
Know this, my lord, nobility of blood
Is but a glittering and fallacious good:
The nobleman is he whose noble mind   [kind.
Is filled with inborn worth, unborrowed from his
The King of Heaven was in a manger laid,
And took his earth but from an humble maid:
Then what can birth, or mortal men, bestow,
Since floods no higher than their fountains flow?
We who for name and empty honour strive
Our true nobility from Him derive.
Your ancestors, who puff your mind with pride
And vast estates to mighty titles tied,
Did not your honour, but their own advance;
But virtue comes not by inheritance.

If you tralineate from your father's mind,
What are you else but of a bastard-kind?
Do as your great progenitors have done,
And by their virtues prove yourself their son.
No father can infuse or wit or grace;
A mother comes across, and mars the race.
A grandsire or a grandame taints the blood;
And seldom three descents continue good.
Were virtue by descent, a noble name
Could never villanise his father's fame:
But, as the first, the last of all the line,
Would, like the sun, even in descending shine.
Take fire, and bear it to the darkest house
Betwixt King Arthur's court and Caucasus;
If you depart, the flame shall still remain,
And the bright blaze enlighten all the plain;
Nor, till the fuel perish, can decay,
By nature formed on things combustible to prey.
Such is not man, who, mixing better seed
With worse, begets a base degenerate breed:
The bad corrupts the good, and leaves behind
No trace of all the great begetter's mind.
The father sinks within his son, we see,
And often rises in the third degree;
If better luck a better mother give,
Chance gave us being, and by chance we live.
Such as our atoms were, even such are we
Or call it Chance, or strong Necessity:
Thus loaded with dead weight, the will is free.
And thus it needs must be: for seed conjoined
Lets into nature's work the imperfect kind;
But fire, the enlivener of the general frame,
Is one, its operation still the same.
Its principle is in itself: while ours
Works, as confederates war, with mingled powers;
Or man or woman, whichsoever fails;
And oft the vigour of the worse prevails.
Æther with sulphur blended alters hue,
And casts a dusky gleam of Sodom blue.
Thus in a brute their ancient honour ends,
And the fair mermaid in a fish descends:

The line is gone; no longer duke or earl;
But, by himself degraded, turns a churl.
Nobility of blood is but renown
Of thy great fathers by their virtue known,
And a long trail of light to thee descending
    down.
If in thy smoke it ends, their glories shine
But infamy and villanage are thine.
Then what I said before is plainly showed,
That true nobility proceeds from God:
Nor left us by inheritance, but given
By bounty of our stars, and grace of Heaven.
Thus from a captive Servius Tullius rose,
Whom for his virtues the first Romans chose:
Fabricius from their walls repelled the foe,
Whose noble hands had exercised the plough.
From hence, my lord and love, I thus conclude,
That though my homely ancestors were rude,
Mean as I am, yet I may have the grace
To make you father of a generous race:
And noble then am I, when I begin,
In virtue clothed, to cast the rags of sin.
If poverty be my upbraided crime,
And you believe in Heaven, there was a time
When He, the great controller of our fate,
Deigned to be man, and lived in low estate;
Which He who had the world at His dispose,
If poverty were vice, would never choose.
Philosophers have said, and poets sing,
That a glad poverty's an honest thing.
Content is wealth, the riches of the mind,
And happy he who can that treasure find;
But the base miser starves amidst his store,
Broods on his gold, and griping still at more,
Sits sadly pining, and believes he's poor.
The ragged beggar, though he wants relief,
Has nought to lose, and sings before the thief.
Want is a bitter and a hateful good,
Because its virtues are not understood.
Yet many things, impossible to thought,
Have been by need to full perfection brought:

The daring of the soul proceeds from thence,
Sharpness of wit, and active diligence ;
Prudence at once and fortitude it gives,
And if in patience taken, mends our lives ;
For even that indigence that brings me low,
Makes me myself and Him above to know ;
A good which none would challenge, few would
A fair possession, which mankind refuse.   [choose :
    If we from wealth to poverty descend,
Want gives to know the flatterer from the friend.
If I am old and ugly, well for you,
No lewd adulterer will my love pursue ;
Nor jealousy, the bane of married life,
Shall haunt you for a withered homely wife ;
For age and ugliness, as all agree,
Are the best guards of female chastity.
    Yet since I see your mind is worldly bent,
I'll do my best to further your content ;
And therefore of two gifts in my dispose,
Think ere you speak, I grant you leave to choose ;
Would you I should be still deformed and old,
Nauseous to touch, and loathsome to behold ;
On this condition to remain for life
A careful, tender, and obedient wife,
In all I can contribute to your ease,
And not in deed, or word, or thought displease?
Or would you rather have me young and fair,
And take the chance that happens to your share ?
Temptations are in beauty, and in youth,
And how can you depend upon my truth ?
Now weigh the danger with the doubtful bliss,
And thank yourself, if aught should fall amiss."
    Sore sighed the knight, who this long sermon
        heard ;
At length considering all, his heart he cheered,
And thus replied :—" My lady, and my wife,
To your wise conduct I resign my life :
Choose you for me, for well you understand
The future good and ill, on either hand :
But if an humble husband may request,
Provide and order all things for the best ;

Yours be the care to profit and to please:
And let your subject-servant take his ease."
   "Then thus in peace," quoth she, "concludes
      the strife,
Since I am turned the husband, you the wife:
The matrimonial victory is mine,
Which, having fairly gained, I will resign;
Forgive if I have said or done amiss,
And seal the bargain with a friendly kiss:
I promised you but one content to share,
But now I will become both good and fair.
No nuptial quarrel shall disturb your ease;
The business of my life shall be to please;
And for my beauty, that, as time shall try,
But draw the curtain first, and cast your eye."
   He looked, and saw a creature heavenly fair,
In bloom of youth, and of a charming air.
With joy he turned, and seized her ivory arm,
And, like Pygmalion, found the statue warm.
Small arguments there needed to prevail,
A storm of kisses poured as thick as hail.
   Thus long in mutual bliss they lay embraced,
And their first love continued to the last:
One sunshine was their life, no cloud between,
Nor ever was a kinder couple seen.
   And so may all our lives like theirs be led;
Heaven send the maids young husbands fresh in bed:
May widows wed as often as they can,
And ever for the better change their man.
And some devouring plague pursue their lives,
Who will not well be governed by their wives.

The Character of a Good Parson.

—·—

A PARISH-PRIEST was of the pilgrim-train;
An awful, reverend, and religious man.
His eyes diffused a venerable grace,
And charity itself was in his face.
Rich was his soul, though his attire was poor,
As God had clothed His own ambassador;
For such on earth his blessed Redeemer bore.
Of sixty years he seemed; and well might last
To sixty more, but that he lived too fast;
Refined himself to soul, to curb the sense
And made almost a sin of abstinence.
Yet had his aspect nothing of severe,
But such a face as promised him sincere.
Nothing reserved or sullen was to see,
But sweet regards, and pleasing sanctity;
Mild was his accent, and his action free.
With eloquence innate his tongue was armed;
Though harsh the precept, yet the preacher charmed:
For, letting down the golden chain from high,
He drew his audience upward to the sky:
And oft with holy hymns he charmed their ears,
A music more melodious than the spheres:
For David left him, when he went to rest,
His lyre; and after him he sung the best.
He bore his great commission in his look:
But sweetly tempered awe, and softened all he spoke.
He preached the joys of heaven and pains of hell,
And warned the sinner with becoming zeal;

But on eternal mercy loved to dwell.
He taught the Gospel rather than the Law ;
And forced himself to drive, but loved to draw.
For fear but freezes minds ; but love, like heat, ·
Exhales the soul sublime, to seek her native seat.

To threats the stubborn sinner oft is hard,
Wrapped in his crimes, against the storm prepared ;
But when the milder beams of mercy play,
He melts, and throws his cumbrous cloak away.

Lightnings and thunder, Heaven's artillery,
As harbingers before the Almighty fly :
Those but proclaim his style, and disappear ;
The stiller sound succeeds, and God is there.

The tithes his parish freely paid he took ;
But never sued, or cursed with bell and book.
With patience bearing wrong, but offering none :
Since every man is free to lose his own.
The country churls, according to their kind,
Who grudge their dues, and love to be behind,
The less he sought his offerings, pinched the more,
And praised a priest contented to be poor.

Yet of his little he had some to spare,
To feed the famished, and to clothe the bare :
For mortified he was to that degree,
A poorer than himself he would not see.
True priests, he said, and preachers of the Word,
Were only stewards of their sovereign Lord,
Nothing was theirs ; but all the public store,
Entrusted riches to relieve the poor ;
Who, should they steal, for want of his relief,
He judged himself accomplice with the thief.

Wide was his parish ; not contracted close
In streets, but here and there a straggling house :
Yet still he was at hand, without request,
To serve the sick, to succour the distressed ;
Tempting, on foot, alone, without affright,
The dangers of a dark tempestuous night.

All this the good old man performed alone,
Nor spared his pains ; for curate he had none.
Nor durst he trust another with his care ;
Nor rode himself to Paul's, the public fair,

To chaffer for preferment with his gold,
Where bishoprics and sinecures are sold ;
But duly watched his flock, by night and day ;
And from the prowling wolf redeemed the prey,
And hungry sent the wily fox away.

The proud he tamed, the penitent he cheered :
Nor to rebuke the rich offender feared.
His preaching much, but more his practice wrought,
A living sermon of the truths he taught ;
For this by rules severe his life he squared :
That all might see the doctrine which they heard.
For priests, he said, are patterns for the rest,
The gold of heaven, who bear the God impressed ;
But when the precious coin is kept unclean,
The sovereign's image is no longer seen.
If they be foul on whom the people trust,
Well may the baser brass contract a rust.

The prelate for his holy life he prized ;
The worldly pomp of prelacy despised.
His Saviour came not with a gaudy show,
Nor was His kingdom of the world below.
Patience in want, and poverty of mind,
These marks of church and churchmen he designed,
And living taught, and dying left behind.
The crown He wore was of the pointed thorn ;
In purple He was crucified, not born.
They who contend for place and high degree,
Are not His sons, but those of Zebedee.

Not but he knew the signs of earthly power
Might well become Saint Peter's successor ;
The holy father holds a double reign,
The prince may keep his pomp, the fisher must be
    plain.

Such was the saint ; who shone with every grace,
Reflecting, Moses-like, his Maker's face.
God saw His image lively was expressed ;
And His own work, as in creation blessed.

The tempter saw him too with envious eye,
And, as on Job, demanded leave to try.
He took the time when Richard was deposed,
And high and low with happy Harry closed.

This prince, though great in arms, the priest with-
 stood,
Near though he was, yet not the next of blood.
Had Richard unconstrained resigned the throne,
A king can give no more than is his own ;
The title stood entailed, had Richard had a son.

Conquest, an odious name, was laid aside ;
Where all submitted, none the battle tried.
The senseless plea of right by Providence
Was by a flattering priest invented since ;
And lasts no longer than the present sway,
But justifies the next who comes in play.

The people's right remains ; let those who dare
Dispute their power, when they the judges are.

He joined not in their choice, because he knew
Worse might and often did from change ensue.
Much to himself he thought ; but little spoke ;
And, undeprived, his benefice forsook.

Now, through the land, his cure of souls he
And like a primitive apostle preached. [stretched,
Still cheerful ; ever constant to his call ;
By many followed ; loved by most, admired by all.
With what he begged, his brethren he relieved !
And gave the charities himself received ;
Gave, while he taught ; and edified the more,
Because he showed by proof 'twas easy to be poor.

He went not with the crowd to see a shrine ;
But fed us by the way with food divine.

In deference to his virtues, I forbear
To show you what the rest in orders were :
This brilliant is so spotless, and so bright,
He needs no foil, but shines by his own proper light.

Sigismonda and Guiscardo.

FROM BOCCACE.

—⁊⧫⧫⧫—

While Norman Tancred in Salerno reigned,
The title of a gracious prince he gained ;
Till turned a tyrant in his latter days,
He lost the lustre of his former praise,
And from the bright meridian where he stood
Descending dipped his hands in lovers' blood.
   This prince, of Fortune's favour long possessed,
Yet was with one fair daughter only blessed ;
And blessed he might have been with her alone,
But oh ! how much more happy had he none !
She was his care, his hope, and his delight,
Most in his thought, and ever in his sight :
Next, nay beyond, his life, he held her dear ;
She lived by him, and now he lived in her.
For this, when ripe for marriage, he delayed
Her nuptial bands, and kept her long a maid,
As envying any else should have a part
Of what was his, and claiming all her heart.
At length, as public decency required,
And all his vassals eagerly desired,
With mind averse, he rather underwent
His people's will than gave his own consent.
So was she torn, as from a lover's side,
And made, almost in his despite, a bride.
   Short were her marriage joys ; for in the prime
Of youth, her lord expired before his time ;
And to her father's court in little space
Restored anew, she held a higher place ;
More loved, and more exalted into grace.

This princess, fresh and young, and fair and wise,
The worshipped idol of her father's eyes.
Did all her sex in every grace exceed,
And had more wit beside than women need.
  Youth, health, and ease, and most an amorous
    mind,
To second nuptials had her thoughts inclined ;
And former joys had left a secret sting behind.
But, prodigal in every other grant,
Her sire left unsupplied her only want ;
And she, betwixt her modesty and pride,
Her wishes, which she could not help, would
    hide.
  Resolved at last to lose no longer time,
And yet to please herself without a crime,
She cast her eyes around the court, to find
A worthy subject suiting to her mind,
To him in holy nuptials to be tied,
A seeming widow and a secret bride.
Among the train of courtiers, one she found
With all the gifts of bounteous nature crowned,
Of gentle blood, but one whose niggard fate
Had set him far below her high estate :
Guiscard his name was called, of blooming age,
Now squire to Tancred, and before his page :
To him, the choice of all the shining crowd,
Her heart the noble Sigismonda vowed.
Yet hitherto she kept her love concealed,
And with close glances every day beheld
The graceful youth ; and every day increased
The raging fire that burned within her breast ;
Some secret charm did all his acts attend,
And what his fortune wanted hers could mend ;
Till, as the fire will force its outward way,
Or, in the prison pent, consume the prey,
So long her earnest eyes on his were set,
At length their twisted rays together met ;
And he, surprised with humble joy, surveyed
One sweet regard, shot by the royal maid.
Not well assured, while doubtful hopes he nursed,
A second glance came gliding like the first ;

And he, who saw the sharpness of the dart,
Without defence received it in his heart.
In public, though their passion wanted speech,
Yet mutual looks interpreted for each :
Time, ways, and means of meeting were denied,
But all those wants ingenious love supplied.
The inventive god, who never fails his part,
Inspires the wit when once he warms the heart.

When Guiscard next was in the circle seen
Where Sigismonda held the place of queen,
A hollow cane within her hand she brought,
But in the concave had enclosed a note ;
With this she seemed to play, and, as in sport,
Tossed to her love in presence of the court ;
"Take it," she said, "and when your needs
        require,
This little brand will serve to light your fire."
He took it with a bow, and soon divined
The seeming toy was not for nought designed :
But when retired, so long with curious eyes
He viewed the present, that he found the prize.
Much was in little writ ; and all conveyed
With cautious care, for fear to be betrayed
By some false confidant or favourite maid.
The time, the place, the manner how to meet,
Were all in punctual order plainly writ :
But since a trust must be, she thought it best
To put it out of laymen's power at least,
And for their solemn vows prepared a priest.

Guiscard, her secret purpose understood,
With joy prepared to meet the coming good ;
Nor pains nor danger was resolved to spare,
But use the means appointed by the fair.

Near the proud palace of Salerno stood
A mount of rough ascent, and thick with wood ;
Through this a cave was dug with vast expense,
The work it seemed of some suspicious prince,
Who, when abusing power with lawless might,
From public justice would secure his flight.
The passage made by many a winding way,
Reached even the room in which the tyrant lay,

Fit for his purpose ; on a lower floor,
He lodged, whose issue was an iron door,
From whence by stairs descending to the ground,
In the blind grot a safe retreat he found.
Its outlet ended in a brake o'ergrown
With brambles, choked by time, and now unknown.
A rift there was, which from the mountain's height
Conveyed a glimmering and malignant light,
A breathing-place to draw the damps away,
A twilight of an intercepted day.
The tyrant's den, whose use though lost to fame,
Was now the apartment of the royal dame ;
The cavern, only to her father known,
By him was to his darling daughter shown.

  Neglected long she let the secret rest,
Till love recalled it to her labouring breast,
And hinted as the way by Heaven designed
The teacher by the means he taught to blind.
What will not women do, when need inspires
Their wit, or love their inclination fires !
Though jealousy of state the invention found,
Yet love refined upon the former ground.
That way the tyrant had reserved, to fly
Pursuing hate, now served to bring two lovers
    nigh.
  The dame, who long in vain had kept the key,
Bold by desire, explored the secret way ;
Now tried the stairs, and wading through the night,
Searched all the deep recess, and issued into light.
All this her letter had so well explained,
The instructed youth might compass what remained;
The cavern-mouth alone was hard to find,
Because the path disused was out of mind :
But in what quarter of the copse it lay,
His eye by certain level could survey :
Yet (for the wood perplexed with thorns he knew)
A frock of leather o'er his limbs he drew ;
And thus provided searched the brake around,
'Till the choked entry of the cave he found.

  Thus all prepared, the promised hour arrived,
So long expected and so well contrived :

With love to friend, the impatient lover went,
Fenced from the thorns, and trod the deep descent.
The conscious priest, who was suborned before,
Stood ready posted at the postern-door ;
The maids in distant rooms were sent to rest,
And nothing wanted but the invited guest.
He came, and, knocking thrice, without delay
The longing lady heard, and turned the key ;
At once invaded him with all her charms,
And the first step he made was in her arms :
The leathern outside, boisterous as it was,
Gave way, and bent beneath her strict embrace :
On either side the kisses flew so thick,
That neither he nor she had breath to speak.
The holy man, amazed at what he saw,
Made haste to sanctify the bliss by law ;
And muttered fast the matrimony o'er,
For fear committed sin should get before.
His work performed, he left the pair alone,
Because he knew he could not go too soon ;
His presence odious, when his task was done.
What thoughts he had beseems not me to say,
Though some surmise he went to fast and pray,
And needed both to drive the tempting thoughts
     away.
   The foe once gone, they took their full delight,
'Twas restless rage and tempest all the night ;
For greedy love each moment would employ,
And grudged the shortest pauses of their joy.
   Thus were their loves auspiciously begun,
And thus with secret care were carried on,
The stealth itself did appetite restore,
And looked so like a sin, it pleased the more.
   The cave was now become a common way,
The wicket, often opened, knew the key.
Love rioted secure, and, long enjoyed,
Was ever eager, and was never cloyed.
   But as extremes are short, of ill and good,
And tides at highest mark regorge the flood ;
So Fate, that could no more improve their joy,
Took a malicious pleasure to destroy.

Tancred, who fondly loved, and whose delight
Was placed in his fair daughter's daily sight,
Of custom, when his state affairs were done.
Would pass his pleasing hours with her alone ;
And, as a father's privilege allowed,
Without attendance of the officious crowd.
   It happened once, that when in heat of day
He tried to sleep, as was his usual way,
The balmy slumber fled his wakeful eyes,
And forced him, in his own despite, to rise :
Of sleep forsaken, to relieve his care,
He sought the conversation of the fair ;
But with her train of damsels she was gone,
In shady walks the scorching heat to shun :
He would not violate that sweet recess,
And found besides a welcome heaviness
That seized his eyes ; and slumber, which forgot,
When called before to come, now came un-
     sought.
From light retired, behind his daughter's bed,
He for approaching sleep composed his head ;
A chair was ready, for that use designed,
So quilted, that he lay at ease reclined ;
The curtains closely drawn, the light to screen.
As if he had contrived to lie unseen :
Thus covered with an artificial night,
Sleep did his office soon, and sealed his night.
   With Heaven averse, in this ill-omened hour
Was Guiscard summoned to the secret bower,
And the fair nymph, with expectation fired,
From her attending damsels was retired :
For, true to love, she measured time so right
As not to miss one moment of delight.
The garden, seated on the level floor,
She left behind, and locking every door,
Thought all secure ; but little did she know,
Blind to her fate, she had enclosed her foe.
Attending Guiscard in his leathern frock
Stood ready with his thrice repeated knock :
Thrice with a doleful sound the jarring grate
Rung deaf and hollow, and presaged their fate.

The door unlocked, to known delight they haste,
And panting, in each other's arms embraced,
Rush to the conscious bed, a mutual freight,
And heedless press it with their wonted weight.
  The sudden bound awaked the sleeping sire,
And showed a sight no parent can desire ;
His opening eyes at once with odious view
The love discovered, and the lover knew :
He would have cried ; but, hoping that he dreamt,
Amazement tied his tongue, and stopped the attempt.
The ensuing moment all the truth declared,
But now he stood collected and prepared ;
For malice and revenge had put him on his guard.
  So, like a lion that unheeded lay,
Dissembling sleep, and watchful to betray,
With inward rage he meditates his prey.
The thoughtless pair, indulging their desires,
Alternate kindled and then quenched their fires ;
Nor thinking in the shades of death they played,
Full of themselves, themselves alone surveyed,
And, too secure, were by themselves betrayed.
Long time dissolved in pleasure thus they lay,
Till nature could no more suffice their play ;
Then rose the youth, and through the cave again
Returned ; the princess mingled with her train.
  Resolved his unripe vengeance to defer,
The royal spy, when now the coast was clear,
Sought not the garden, but retired unseen,
To brood in secret on his gathered spleen,
And methodise revenge : to death he grieved ;
And, but he saw the crime, had scarce believed.
The appointment for the ensuing night he heard ;
And, therefore, in the cavern had prepared
Two brawny yeomen of his trusty guard.
  Scarce had unwary Guiscard set his foot
Within the foremost entrance of the grot,
When these in secret ambush ready lay,
And, rushing on the sudden, seized the prey.
Encumbered with his frock, without defence,
An easy prize, they led the prisoner thence,
And, as commanded, brought before the prince.

The gloomy sire, too sensible of wrong
To vent his rage in words, restrained his tongue,
And only said, "Thus servants are preferred
And trusted, thus their sovereigns they reward :
Had I not seen, had not these eyes received
Too clear a proof, I could not have believed."
    He paused, and choked the rest. The youth, who
His forfeit life abandoned to the law,   [saw
The judge the accuser, and the offence to him
Who had both power and will to avenge the crime,
No vain defence prepared, but thus replied :
"'The faults of love by love are justified ;
With unresisted might the monarch reigns,
He levels mountains, and he raises plains,
And, not regarding difference of degree,
Abased your daughter and exalted me.."
    This bold return with seeming patience heard,
The prisoner was remitted to the guard.
The sullen tyrant slept not all the night,
But lonely walking by a winking light,
Sobbed, wept, and groaned, and beat his withered
But would not violate his daughter's rest ;   [breast,
Who long expecting lay, for bliss prepared,
Listening for noise, and grieved that none she heard ;
Oft rose, and oft in vain employed the key,
And oft accused her lover of delay,
And passed the tedious hours in anxious thoughts
      away.
    The morrow came ; and at his usual hour,
Old Tancred visited his daughter's bower ;
Her cheek (for such his custom was) he kissed,
Then blessed her kneeling, and her maids dismissed.
The royal dignity thus far maintained,
Now left in private, he no longer feigned ;
But all at once his grief and rage appeared,
And floods of tears ran trickling down his beard.
    "O Sigismonda," he began to say ;
Thrice he began, and thrice was forced to stay,
Till words with often trying found their way ;
"I thought, O Sigismonda (but how blind
Are parents' eyes their children's faults to find !),

Thy virtue, birth, and breeding were above
A mean desire, and vulgar sense of love ;
Nor less than sight and hearing could convince
So fond a father, and so just a prince,
Of such an unforeseen and unbelieved offence :
Then what indignant sorrow must I have,
To see thee lie subjected to my slave !
A man so smelling of the people's lee,
The court received him first for charity ;
And since with no degree of honour graced,
But only suffered where he first was placed ;
A grovelling insect still ; and so designed
By nature's hand, nor born of noble kind ;
A thing by neither man nor woman prized,
And scarcely known enough to be despised :
To what has Heaven reserved my age?   Ah ! why
Should man, when nature calls, not choose to die ;
Rather than stretch the span of life, to find
Such ills as Fate has wisely cast behind,
For those to feel, whom fond desire to live
Makes covetous of more than life can give !
Each has his share of good ; and when 'tis gone,
The guest, though hungry, cannot rise too soon.
But I, expecting more, in my own wrong
Protracting life, have lived a day too long.
If yesterday could be recalled again,
Even now would I conclude my happy reign ;
But 'tis too late, my glorious race is run,
And a dark cloud o'ertakes my setting sun.
Hadst thou not loved, or loving saved the shame,
If not the sin, by some illustrious name,
This little comfort had relieved my mind,
'Twas frailty, not unusual to thy kind :
But thy low fall beneath thy royal blood
Shows downward appetite to mix with mud.
Thus not the least excuse is left for thee,
Nor the least refuge for unhappy me.
    For him I have resolved : whom by surprise
I took, and scarce can call it, in disguise ;
For such was his attire, as, with intent
Of nature, suited to his mean descent :

The harder question yet remains behind,
What pains a parent and a prince can find
To punish an offence of this degenerate kind.
   As I have loved, and yet I love thee more
Than ever father loved a child before ;
So that indulgence draws me to forgive :
Nature, that gave thee life, would have thee liv
But, as a public parent of the state,
My justice and thy crime requires thy fate.
Fain would I choose a middle course to steer ;
Nature's too kind, and justice too severe :
Speak for us both, and to the balance bring
On either side the father and the king.
Heaven knows, my heart is bent to favour thee
Make it but scanty weight, and leave the r
    to me."
   Here stopping with a sigh, he poured a flood
Of tears, to make his last expression good.
   She who had heard him speak, nor saw alone
The secret conduct of her love was known,
But he was taken who her soul possessed,
Felt all the pangs of sorrow in her breast :
And little wanted, but a woman's heart
With cries and tears had testified her smart,
But inborn worth, that fortune can control,
New strung and stiffer bent her softer soul ;
The heroine assumed the woman's place,
Confirmed her mind, and fortified her face :
Why should she beg, or what could she pretend
When her stern father had condemned her frien
Her life she might have had ; but her despair
Of saving his had put it past her care :
Resolved on fate, she would not lose her breath
But, rather than not die, solicit death.
Fixed on this thought, she, not as women use,
Her fault by common frailty would excuse ;
But boldly justified her innocence,
And while the fact was owned, denied the offen
Then with dry eyes, and with an open look,
She met his glance midway, and thus undaun'
    spoke :

" Tancred, I neither am disposed to make
Request for life, nor offered life to take ;
Much less deny the deed ; but least of all
Beneath pretended justice weakly fall.
My words to sacred truth shall be confined,
My deeds shall show the greatness of my mind.
That I have loved, I own ; that still I love
I call to witness all the powers above:
Yet more I own ; to Guiscard's love I give
The small remaining time I have to live ;
And if beyond this life desire can be,
Not Fate itself shall set my passion free.

  This first avowed, nor folly warped my mind,
Nor the frail texture of the female kind
Betrayed my virtue ; for too well I knew
What honour was, and honour had his due :
Before the holy priest my vows were tied,
So came I not a strumpet, but a bride :
This for my fame and for the public voice ;
Yet more, his merits justified my choice :
Which had they not, the first election thine,
That bond dissolved, the next is freely mine ;
Or grant I erred (which yet I must deny),
Had parents power even second vows to tie,
Thy little care to mend my widowed nights
Has forced me to recourse of marriage rites,
To fill an empty side, and follow known delights.
What have I done in this, deserving blame?
State laws may alter : nature's are the same ;
Those are usurped on helpless womankind,
Made without our consent, and wanting power
    to bind.
Thou, Tancred, better shouldst have understood,
That, as thy father gave thee flesh and blood,
So gavest thou me : not from the quarry hewed,
But of a softer mould, with sense endued ;
Even softer than thy own, of suppler kind,
More exquisite of taste, and more than man refined.
Nor needst thou by thy daughter to be told,
Though now thy sprightly blood with age be
    cold,

G

Thou hast been young: and canst remember still,
That when thou hadst the power, thou hadst the
And from the past experience of thy fires,　[will:
Canst tell with what a tide our strong desires
Come rushing on in youth, and what their rage
　requires.
　And grant thy youth was exercised in arms,
When love no leisure found for softer charms,
My tender age in luxury was trained,
With idle ease and pageants entertained;
My hours my own, my pleasures unrestrained.
So bred, no wonder if I took the bent
That seemed even warranted by thy consent,
For, when the father is too fondly kind,
Such seed he sows, such harvest shall he find.
Blame then thyself, as reason's law requires
(Since nature gave and thou foment'st my fires);
If still those appetites continue strong,
Thou may'st consider I am yet but young.
Consider too that, having been a wife,
I must have tasted of a better life,
And am not to be blamed, if I renew
By lawful means the joys which then I knew.
Where was the crime, if pleasure I procured,
Young, and a woman, and to bliss inured?
That was my case, and this is my defence:
I pleased myself, I shunned incontinence,
And, urged by strong desires, indulged my sense.
　Left to myself, I must avow, I strove
From public shame to screen my secret love,
And, well acquainted with thy native pride,
Endeavoured what I could not help to hide,
For which a woman's wit an easy way supplied.
How this, so well contrived, so closely laid,
Was known to thee, or by what chance betrayed,
Is not my care; to please thy pride alone,
I could have wished it had been still unknown.
　Nor took I Guiscard, by blind fancy led
Or hasty choice, as many women wed;
But with deliberate care, and ripened thought,
At leisure first designed, before I wrought:

On him I rested after long debate,
And not without considering fixed my fate:
His flame was equal, though by mine inspired
(For so the difference of our birth required):
Had he been born like me, like me his love
Had first begun what mine was forced to move:
But thus beginning, thus we persevere;
Our passions yet continue what they were,
Nor length of trial makes our joys the less sincere.

  At this my choice, though not by thine allowed
(Thy judgment herding with the common crowd),
Thou tak'st unjust offence; and, led by them,
Dost less the merit than the man esteem.
Too sharply, Tancred, by thy pride betrayed,
Hast thou against the laws of kind inveighed;
For all the offence is in opinion placed,
Which deems high birth by lowly choice debased.
This thought alone with fury fires thy breast
(For holy marriage justifies the rest),
That I have sunk the glories of the state,
And mixed my blood with a plebeian mate:
In which I wonder thou shouldst oversee
Superior causes, or impute to me
The fault of Fortune, or the Fates' decree.
Or call it Heaven's imperial power alone, [known.
Which moves on springs of justice, though un-
Yet this we see, though ordered for the best,
The bad exalted, and the good oppressed;
Permitted laurels grace the lawless brow,
The unworthy raised, the worthy cast below.

  But leaving that: search we the secret springs,
And backward trace the principles of things;
There shall we find, that when the world began,
One common mass composed the mould of man;
One paste of flesh on all degrees bestowed,
And kneaded up alike with moistening blood.
The same Almighty Power inspired the frame
With kindled life, and formed the souls the same:
The faculties of intellect and will
Dispensed with equal hand, disposed with equal skill,
Like liberty indulged with choice of good or ill.

Thus born alike, from virtue first began
The difference that distinguished man from man :
He claimed no title from descent of blood,
But that which made him noble made him good.
Warmed with more particles of heavenly flame,
He winged his upward flight, and soared to fame ;
The rest remained below, a tribe without a name.
    This law, though custom now diverts the course,
As nature's institute, is yet in force ;
Uncancelled, though disused ; and he, whose mind
Is virtuous, is alone of noble kind ;
Though poor in fortune, of celestial race ;
And he commits the crime who calls him base.
    Now lay the line ; and measure all thy court
By inward virtue, not external port,
And find whom justly to prefer above
The man on whom my judgment placed my love ;
So shalt thou see his parts and person shine,
And thus compared, the rest a base degenerate line.
Nor took I, when I first surveyed thy court,
His valour or his virtues on report ;
But trusted what I ought to trust alone,
Relying on thy eyes, and not my own ;
Thy praise (and thine was then the public voice)
First recommended Guiscard to my choice :
Directed thus by thee, I looked, and found
A man I thought deserving to be crowned !
First by my father pointed to my sight,
Nor less conspicuous by his native light ;
His mind, his mien, the features of his face,
Excelling all the rest of human race :   [aright,
These were thy thoughts, and thou couldst judge
Till interest made a jaundice in thy sight.
    Or should I grant thou didst not rightly see,
Then thou wert first deceived, and I deceived by thee.
But if thou shalt allege, through pride of mind,
Thy blood with one of base condition joined,
'Tis false ; for 'tis not baseness to be poor :
His poverty augments thy crime the more ;
Upbraids thy justice with the scant regard
Of worth ; whom princes praise, they should reward.

Are these the kings entrusted by the crowd
With wealth, to be dispensed for common good?
The people sweat not for their king's delight
To enrich a pimp, or raise a parasite;
Theirs is the toil; and he who well has served
His country, has his country's wealth deserved.
  Even mighty monarchs oft are meanly born,
And kings by birth to lowest rank return;
All subject to the power of giddy chance,
For Fortune can depress, or can advance;
But true nobility is of the mind,
Not given by chance, and not to chance resigned.
  For the remaining doubt of thy decree,
What to resolve, and how dispose of me,
Be warned to cast that useless care aside,
Myself alone will for myself provide.
If in thy doting and decrepit age,
Thy soul, a stranger in thy youth to rage,
Begins in cruel deeds to take delight,
Gorge with my blood thy barbarous appetite;
For I so little am disposed to pray
For life, I would not cast a wish away.
Such as it is, the offence is all my own;
And what to Guiscard is already done,
Or to be done is doomed by thy decree,
That, if not executed first by thee,
Shall on my person be performed by me.
  Away! with women weep, and leave me here,
Fixed, like a man, to die without a tear;
Or save or slay us both this present hour,
'Tis all that Fate has left within thy power."
She said; nor did her father fail to find
In all she spoke the greatness of her mind;
Yet thought she was not obstinate to die,
Nor deemed the death she promised was so nigh:
Secure in this belief, he left the dame,
Resolved to spare her life, and save her shame;
But that detested object to remove,
To wreak his vengeance, and to cure her love.
  Intent on this, a secret order signed
The death of Guiscard to his guards enjoined:

Strangling was chosen, and the night the time ;
A mute revenge, and blind as was the crime :
His faithful heart, a bloody sacrifice,
Torn from his breast, to glut the tyrant's eyes,
Closed the severe command ; for, slaves to pay,
What kings decree the soldier must obey :
Waged against foes, and, when the wars are o'er,
Fit only to maintain despotic power ;
Dangerous to freedom, and desired alone
By kings who seek an arbitrary throne.
Such were these guards ; as ready to have slain
The Prince himself, allured with greater gain ;
So was the charge performed with better will,
By men inured to blood, and exercised in ill.
　Now, though the sullen sire had eased his mind,
The pomp of his revenge was still behind,
A pomp prepared to grace the present he designed.
A goblet rich with gems, and rough with gold,
Of depth and breadth the precious pledge to hold,
With cruel care he chose ; the hollow part
Enclosed, the lid concealed the lover's heart.
Then of his trusted mischiefs one he sent,
And bade him, with these words, the gift present :
" Thy father sends thee this to cheer thy breast,
And glad thy sight with what thou lov'st the best,
As thou hast pleased his eyes, and joyed his mind,
With what he loved the most of human kind."
　Ere this, the royal dame, who well had weighed
The consequence of what her sire had said,
Fixed on her fate, against the expected hour,
Procured the means to have it in her power ;
For this she had distilled with early care
The juice of simples friendly to despair,
A magazine of death, and thus prepared,
Secure to die, the fatal message heard :
Then smiled severe ; nor with a troubled look,
Or trembling hand, the funeral present took ;
Even kept her countenance, when the lid removed
Disclosed the heart, unfortunately loved.
She needed not be told within whose breast
It lodged ; the message had explained the rest.

Or not amazed, or hiding her surprise,
She sternly on the bearer fixed her eyes;
Then thus: "Tell Tancred, on his daughter's
  part,
The gold, though precious, equals not the heart;
But he did well to give his best; and I,
Who wished a worthier urn, forgive his poverty."
  At this she curbed a groan, that else had come,
And pausing, viewed the present in the tomb;
Then to the heart adored devoutly glued
Her lips, and raising it, her speech renewed:
"Even from my day of birth, to this, the bound
Of my unhappy being, I have found
My father's care and tenderness expressed;
But this last act of love excels the rest:
For this so dear a present, bear him back
The best return that I can live to make."
  The messenger despatched, again she viewed
The loved remains, and, sighing, thus pursued:
"Source of my life, and lord of my desires,
In whom I lived, with whom my soul expires!
Poor heart, no more the spring of vital heat,
Cursed be the hands that tore thee from thy seat!
The course is finished which thy fates decreed,
And thou from thy corporeal prison freed:
Soon hast thou reached the goal with mended
  pace;
A world of woes despatched in little space;
Forced by thy worth, thy foe, in death become
Thy friend, has lodged thee in a costly tomb.
There yet remained thy funeral exequies,
The weeping tribute of thy widow's eyes;
And those indulgent Heaven has found the way
That I, before my death, have leave to pay.
My father even in cruelty is kind,
Or Heaven has turned the malice of his mind
To better uses than his hate designed,
And made the insult, which in his gift appears,
The means to mourn thee with my pious tears;
Which I will pay thee down before I go,
And save myself the pains to weep below,

If souls can weep. Though once I meant to meet
My fate with face unmoved, and eyes unwet,
Yet, since I have thee here in narrow room,
My tears shall set thee first afloat within thy tomb.
Then (as I know thy spirit hovers nigh)
Under thy friendly conduct will I fly
To regions unexplored, secure to share
Thy state ; nor hell shall punishment appear ;
And heaven is double heaven, if thou art there."
   She said.   Her brimful eyes, that ready stood,
And only wanted will to weep a flood,
Released their watery store, and poured amain,
Like clouds low hung, a sober shower of rain ;
Mute solemn sorrow, free from female noise,
Such as the majesty of grief destroys ;
For, bending o'er the cup, the tears she shed
Seemed by the posture to discharge her head,
O'erfilled before ; and oft (her mouth applied
To the cold heart) she kissed at once and cried.
Her maids, who stood amazed, nor knew the cause
Of her complaining, nor whose heart it was,
Yet all due measures of her mourning kept,
Did office at the dirge, and by infection wept,
And oft inquired the occasion of her grief,
Unanswered but by sighs, and offered vain relief.
At length, her stock of tears already shed,
She wiped her eyes, she raised her drooping head,
And thus pursued :—" O ever faithful heart,
I have performed the ceremonial part,
The decencies of grief ; it rests behind,
That as our bodies were, our souls be joined ;
To thy whate'er abode my shade convey,
And, as an elder ghost, direct the way !"
She said ; and bade the vial to be brought,
Where she before had brewed the deadly draught :
First pouring out the med'cinable bane,
The heart her tears had rinsed she bathed again ;

Then down her throat the death securely throws,
And quaffs a long oblivion of her woes.
  This done, she mounts the genial bed, and there
(Her body first composed with honest care)
Attends the welcome rest ; her hands yet hold
Close to her heart the monumental gold ;
No further word she spoke, but closed her sight,
And quiet sought the covert of the night.
  The damsels, who the while in silence mourned,
Not knowing nor suspecting death suborned,
Yet, as their duty was, to Tancred sent,
Who, conscious of the occasion, feared the event.
Alarmed, and with presaging heart, he came
And drew the curtains, and exposed the dame
To loathsome light ; then with a late relief
Made vain efforts to mitigate her grief.
She, what she could, excluding day, her eyes
Kept firmly sealed, and sternly thus replies :
  " Tancred, restrain thy tears unsought by me,
And sorrow unavailing now to thee :
Did ever man before afflict his mind
To see the effect of what himself designed ?
Yet, if thou hast remaining in thy heart
Some sense of love, some unextinguished part
Of former kindness, largely once professed,
Let me by that adjure thy hardened breast
Not to deny thy daughter's last request :
The secret love which I so long enjoyed,
And still concealed to gratify thy pride,
Thou hast disjoined ; but, with my dying breath,
Seek not, I beg thee, to disjoin our death :
Where'er his corpse by thy command is laid,
Thither let mine in public be conveyed ;
Exposed in open view, and side by side,
Acknowledged as a bridegroom and a bride."
  The Prince's anguish hindered his reply ;
And she, who felt her fate approaching nigh,
Seized the cold heart, and heaving to her breast,
" Here, precious pledge," she said, " securely rest."
These accents were her last ; the creeping death
Benumbed her senses first, then stopped her breath.

Thus she for disobedience justly died ;
The sire was justly punished for his pride ;
The youth, least guilty, suffered for the offence
Of duty violated to his Prince ;
Who, late repenting of his cruel deed,
One common sepulchre for both decreed ;
Entombed the wretched pair in royal state,
And on their monument inscribed their fate.

Theodore and Honoria

FROM BOCCACE.

Of all the cities in Romanian lands,
The chief and most renowned Ravenna stands ;
Adorned in ancient times with arms and arts,
And rich inhabitants with generous hearts.
But Theodore the brave, above the rest,
With gifts of fortune and of nature blessed,
The foremost place for wealth and honour held,
And all in feats of chivalry excelled.
  This noble youth to madness loved a dame
Of high degree, Honoria was her name ;
Fair as the fairest, but of haughty mind,
And fiercer than became so soft a kind ;
Proud of her birth (for equal she had none),
The rest she scorned, but hated him alone ;
His gifts, his constant courtship, nothing gained :
For she, the more he loved, the more disdained.
He lived with all the pomp he could devise,
At tilts and tournaments obtained the prize,
But found no favour in his lady's eyes :
Relentless as a rock, the lofty maid
Turned all to poison that he did or said :
Nor prayers nor tears nor offered vows could move :
The work went backward ; and the more he strove
To advance his suit, the farther from her love.
  Wearied at length, and wanting remedy,
He doubted oft, and oft resolved to die.
But pride stood ready to prevent the blow,
For who would die to gratify a foe?
His generous mind disdained so mean a fate ;
That passed, his next endeavour was to hate.

But vainer that relief than all the rest ;
The less he hoped, with more desire possessed ;
Love stood the siege, and would not yield his breast.
  Change was the next, but change deceived his
He sought a fairer, but found none so fair.   [care;
He would have worn her out by slow degrees,
As men by fasting starve the untamed disease ;
But present love required a present ease.
Looking, he feeds alone his famished eyes,
Feeds lingering death, but, looking not, he dies.
Yet still he chose the longest way to fate,
Wasting at once his life and his estate.
  His friends beheld, and pitied him in vain,
For what advice can ease a lover's pain ?
Absence, the best expedient they could find,
Might save the fortune, if not cure the mind :
This means they long proposed, but little gained,
Yet after much pursuit at length obtained.
  Hard you may think it was to give consent,
But struggling with his own desires he went ;
With large expense, and with a pompous train,
Provided as to visit France or Spain,
Or for some distant voyage o'er the main.
But love had clipped his wings, and cut him short,
Confined within the purlieus of his court.
Three miles he went, nor farther could retreat ;
His travels ended at his country seat :
To Chassi's pleasing plains he took his way,
There pitched his tents, and there resolved to stay.
  The spring was in the prime, the neighbouring
Supplied with birds, the choristers of love ;   [grove
Music unbought, that ministered delight
To morning walks, and lulled his cares by night :
There he discharged his friends, but not the expense
Of frequent treats and proud magnificence.
He lived as kings retire, though more at large
From public business, yet with equal charge ;
With house and heart still open to receive ;
As well content as love would give him leave :
He would have lived more free ; but many a guest,
Who could forsake the friend, pursued the feast.

It happed one morning, as his fancy led,
Before his usual hour he left his bed,
To walk within a lonely lawn, that stood
On every side surrounded by the wood :
Alone he walked, to please his pensive mind,
And sought the deepest solitude to find ;
'Twas in a grove of spreading pines he strayed ;
The winds within the quivering branches played,
And dancing trees a mournful music made ;
The place itself was suiting to his care,
Uncouth and savage as the cruel fair.
He wandered on, unknowing where he went,
Lost in the wood, and all on love intent :
The day already half his race had run,
And summoned him to due repast at noon,
But love could feel no hunger but his own.

While listening to the murmuring leaves he stood,
More than a mile immersed within the wood,
At once the wind was laid ; the whispering sound
Was dumb ; a rising earthquake rocked the ground;
With deeper brown the grove was overspread,
A sudden horror seized his giddy head,
And his ears tingled, and his colour fled.
Nature was in alarm ; some danger nigh
Seemed threatened, though unseen to mortal eye.
Unused to fear, he summoned all his soul,
And stood collected in himself—and whole ;
Not long : for soon a whirlwind rose around,
And from afar he heard a screaming sound,
As of a dame distressed, who cried for aid,
And filled with loud laments the secret shade.

A thicket close beside the grove there stood,
With briers and brambles choked, and dwarfish
        wood ;
From thence the noise, which now approaching near
With more distinguished notes invades his ear ;
He raised his head, and saw a beauteous maid
With hair dishevelled issuing through the shade ;
Stripped of her clothes, and e'en those parts re-
        vealed
Which modest nature keeps from sight concealed.

Her face, her hands, her naked limbs were torn,
With passing through the brakes and prickly thorn;
Two mastiffs gaunt and grim her flight pursued,
And oft their fastened fangs in blood imbrued:
Oft they came up, and pinched her tender side,
" Mercy, O mercy, Heaven," she ran, and cried:
When Heaven was named they loosed their hold
 again,
Then sprung she forth, they followed her amain.
 Not far behind, a knight of swarthy face
High on a coal-black steed pursued the chase;
With flashing flames his ardent eyes were filled,
And in his hand a naked sword he held:
He cheered the dogs to follow her who fled,
And vowed revenge on her devoted head.
 As Theodore was born of noble kind,
The brutal action roused his manly mind:
Moved with unworthy usage of the maid,
He, though unarmed, resolved to give her aid.
A sapling pine he wrenched from out the ground,
The readiest weapon that his fury found.
Thus, furnished for offence, he crossed the way
Betwixt the graceless villain and his prey.
 The knight came thundering on, but, from afar,
Thus in imperious tone forbade the war:
"Cease, Theodore, to proffer vain relief,
Nor stop the vengeance of so just a grief;
But give me leave to seize my destined prey,
And let eternal justice take the way:
I but revenge my fate, disdained, betrayed,
And suffering death for this ungrateful maid."
 He said, at once dismounting from the steed;
For now the hell-hounds with superior speed
Had reached the dame, and, fastening on her side,
The ground with issuing streams of purple dyed.
Stood Theodore surprised in deadly fright,
With chattering teeth, and bristling hair upright;
Yet armed with inborn worth,—"Whate'er," said he,
"Thou art, who knowest me better than I thee;
Or prove thy rightful cause, or be defied."
The spectre fiercely staring, thus replied:

" Know, Theodore, thy ancestry I claim,
And Guido Cavalcanti was my name.
One common sire our fathers did beget,
My name and story some remember yet ;
Thee, then a boy, within my arms I laid,
When for my sins I loved this haughty maid ;
Not less adored in life, nor served by me,
Than proud Honoria now is loved by thee.
What did I not her stubborn heart to gain?
But all my vows were answered with disdain :
She scorned my sorrows, and despised my pain.
Long time I dragged my days in fruitless care ;
Then loathing life, and plunged in deep despair,
To finish my unhappy life I fell
On this sharp sword, and now am damned in hell.
  Short was her joy ; for soon the insulting maid
By Heaven's decree in the cold grave was laid ;
And as in unrepenting sin she died,
Doomed to the same bad place, is punished for
      her pride :
Because she deemed I well deserved to die,
And made a merit of her cruelty.
There, then, we met ; both tried, and both were
      cast,
And this irrevocable sentence passed,
That, she whom I so long pursued in vain,
Should suffer from my hands a lingering pain :
Renewed to life, that she might daily die,
I daily doomed to follow, she to fly ;
No more a lover, but a mortal foe,
I seek her life (for love is none below) ;
As often as my dogs with better speed
Arrest her flight, is she to death decreed :
Then with this fatal sword, on which I died,
I pierce her opened back or tender side,
And tear that hardened heart from out her breast,
Which with her entrails makes my hungry hounds
      a feast.
Nor lies she long, but as her fates ordain,
Springs up to life, and fresh to second pain,
Is saved to-day, to-morrow to be slain."

This, versed in death, the infernal knight relates,
And then for proof fulfilled their common fates;
Her heart and bowels through her back he drew,
And fed the hounds that helped him to pursue.
Stern looked the fiend, as frustrate of his will,
Not half sufficed, and greedy yet to kill.
And now the soul, expiring through the wound,
Had left the body breathless on the ground,
When thus the grisly spectre spoke again:
" Behold the fruit of ill-rewarded pain !
As many months as I sustained her hate,
So many years is she condemned by Fate
To daily death; and every several place
Conscious of her disdain and my disgrace,
Must witness her just punishment, and be
A scene of triumph and revenge to me.
As in this grove I took my last farewell,
As on this very spot of earth I fell,
As Friday saw me die, so she my prey
Becomes even here, on this revolving day."
    Thus while he spoke, the virgin from the ground
Upstarted fresh, already closed the wound,
And unconcerned for all she felt before,
Precipitates her flight along the shore:
The hell-hounds, as ungorged with flesh and blood,
Pursue their prey, and seek their wonted food:
The fiend remounts his courser, mends his pace,
And all the vision vanished from the place.
    Long stood the noble youth oppressed with awe
And stupid at the wondrous things he saw,
Surpassing common faith, transgressing nature's
    law.
He would have been asleep, and wished to wake,
But dreams, he knew, no long impression make,
Though strong at first; if vision, to what end,
But such as must his future state portend,
His love the damsel, and himself the fiend?
But yet reflecting that it could not be
From Heaven, which cannot impious acts decree,
Resolved within himself to shun the snare
Which hell for his destruction did prepare;

And as his better genius should direct,
From an ill cause to draw a good effect.
   Inspired from Heaven he homeward took his way,
Nor palled his new design with long delay,
But of his train a trusty servant sent
To call his friends together at his tent.
They came, and, usual salutations paid,
With words premeditated thus he said:
" What you have often counselled, to remove
My vain pursuit of unregarded love,
By thrift my sinking fortune to repair,
Though late, yet is at last become my care:
My heart shall be my own; my vast expense
Reduced to bounds by timely providence:
This only I require; invite for me
Honoria, with her father's family,
Her friends and mine; the cause I shall display,
On Friday next, for that's the appointed day."
   Well pleased were all his friends, the task was
The father, mother, daughter they invite;   [light,
Hardly the dame was drawn to this repast;
But yet resolved, because it was the last.
The day was come, the guests invited came,
And with the rest the inexorable dame:
A feast prepared with riotous expense,
Much cost, more care, and most magnificence.
The place ordained was in that haunted grove
Where the revenging ghost pursued his love:
The tables in a proud pavilion spread,
With flowers below, and tissue overhead:
The rest in rank, Honoria, chief in place,
Was artfully contrived to set her face
To front the thicket and behold the chase.
The feast was served, the time so well forecast
That just when the dessert and fruits were placed,
The fiend's alarm began; the hollow sound
Sung in the leaves, the forest shook around,
Air blackened, rolled the thunder, groaned the
      ground.
   Nor long before the loud laments arise
Of one distressed, and mastiffs' mingled cries;

And first the dame came rushing through the wood,
And next the famished hounds that sought their
 food,
And griped her flanks, and oft essayed their jaws in
Last came the felon on the sable steed,   [blood.
Armed with his naked sword, and urged his dogs
 to speed.
She ran, and cried, her flight directly bent
(A guest unbidden) to the fatal tent,   [ment.
The scene of death, and place ordained for punish-
Loud was the noise, aghast was every guest,
The women shrieked, the men forsook the feast ;
The hounds at nearer distance hoarsely bayed ;
The hunter close pursued the visionary maid,
She rent the heaven with loud laments, imploring
 The gallants, to protect the lady's right, [aid.
Their faulchions brandished at the grisly spright ;
High on his stirrups he provoked the fight.
Then on the crowd he cast a furious look,
And withered all their strength before he strook :
" Back on your lives ! let be," said he, " my prey,
And let my vengeance take the destined way :
Vain are your arms, and vainer your defence,
Against the eternal doom of Providence :
Mine is the ungrateful maid by Heaven designed :
Mercy she would not give, nor mercy shall she find."
At this the former tale again he told
With thundering tone, and dreadful to behold :
Sunk were their hearts with horror of the crime,
Nor needed to be warned a second time,
But bore each other back ; some knew the face,
And all had heard the much lamented case
Of him who fell for love, and this the fatal place.
 And now the infernal minister advanced,
Seized the due victim, and with fury lanced
Her back, and piercing through her inmost heart,
Drew backward as before the offending part.
The reeking entrails next he tore away,
And to his meagre mastiffs made a prey.
The pale assistants on each other stared,
With gaping mouths for issuing words prepared ;

The stillborn sounds upon the palate hung,
And died imperfect on the faltering tongue.
The fright was general; but the female band,
A helpless train, in more confusion stand:
With horror shuddering, on a heap they run,
Sick at the sight of hateful justice done;
For conscience rung the alarm, and made the case
　　their own.
　So spread upon a lake, with upward eye,
A plump of fowl behold their foe on high;
They close their trembling troop; and all attend
On whom the sowsing eagle will descend.
　But most the proud Honoria feared the event,
And thought to her alone the vision sent.
Her guilt presents to her distracted mind
Heaven's justice, Theodore's revengeful kind,
And the same fate to the same sin assigned;
Already sees herself the monster's prey,
And feels her heart and entrails torn away.
'Twas a mute scene of sorrow, mixed with fear;
Still on the table lay the unfinished cheer:
The knight and hungry mastiffs stood around,
The mangled dame lay breathless on the ground;
When on a sudden, re-inspired with breath,
Again she rose, again to suffer death;
Nor stayed the hell-hounds, nor the hunter stayed,
But followed, as before, the flying maid:
The avenger took from earth the avenging sword,
And mounting light as air his sable steed he
　　spurred:
The clouds dispelled, the sky resumed her light,
And nature stood recovered of her fright.
　But fear, the last of ills, remained behind,
And horror heavy sat on every mind.
Nor Theodore encouraged more his feast,
But sternly looked, as hatching in his breast
Some deep design, which when Honoria viewed
The fresh impulse her former fright renewed:
She thought herself the trembling dame who fled,
And him the grisly ghost that spurred the infernal
　　steed:

The more dismayed, for when the guests withdrew,
Their courteous host saluting all the crew,
Regardless passed her o'er, nor graced with kind
    adieu.
That sting infixed within her haughty mind,
The downfall of her empire she divined ;
And her proud heart with secret sorrow pined.
Home as they went, the sad discourse renewed,
Of the relentless dame to death pursued,
And of the sight obscene so lately viewed ;
None durst arraign the righteous doom she bore,
Even they who pitied most yet blamed her more :
The parallel they needed not to name,
But in the dead they damned the living dame.
   At every little noise she looked behind,
For still the knight was present to her mind :
And anxious oft she started on the way,
And thought the horseman-ghost came thundering
    for his prey.
Returned, she took her bed with little rest,
But in short slumbers dreamt the funeral feast :
Awaked, she turned her side, and slept again ;
The same black vapours mounted in her brain,
And the same dreams returned with double pain.
   Now forced to wake, because afraid to sleep,
Her blood all fevered, with a furious leap
She sprung from bed, distracted in her mind,
And feared, at every step, a twitching spright
    behind.
Darkling and desperate, with a staggering pace,
Of death afraid, and conscious of disgrace,
Fear, pride, remorse, at once her heart assailed ;
Pride put remorse to flight, but fear prevailed.
Friday, the fatal day, when next it came,
Her soul forethought the fiend would change his
    game,'
And her pursue, or Theodore be slain,
And two ghosts join their packs to hunt her o'er
    the plain.
   This dreadful image so possessed her mind,
That, desperate any succour else to find,

She ceased all further hope; and now began
To make reflection on the unhappy man.
Rich, brave, and young, who past expression loved,
Proof to disdain, and not to be removed:
Of all the men respected and admired,
Of all the dames, except herself, desired:
Why not of her? preferred above the rest
By him with knightly deeds, and open love pro-
    fessed?
So had another been, where he his vows addressed.
This quelled her pride, yet other doubts remained,
That once disdaining, she might be disdained.
The fear was just, but greater fear prevailed,
Fear of her life by hellish hounds assailed:
He took a lowering leave; but who can tell
What outward hate might inward love conceal?
Her sex's arts she knew, and why not then
Might deep dissembling have a place in men?
Here hope began to dawn; resolved to try,
She fixed on this her utmost remedy;
Death was behind, but hard it was to die:
'Twas time enough at last on death to call;
The precipice in sight, a shrub was all
That kindly stood betwixt to break the fatal fall.
    One maid she had, beloved above the rest:
Secure of her, the secret she confessed;
And now the cheerful light her fears dispelled,
She with no winding turns the truth concealed,
But put the woman off, and stood revealed:
With faults confessed, commissioned her to go,
If pity yet had place, and reconcile her foe.
The welcome message made was soon received;
'Twas what he wished and hoped, but scarce
    believed:
Fate seemed a fair occasion to present,
He knew the sex, and feared she might repent
Should he delay the moment of consent.
There yet remained to gain her friends (a care
The modesty of maidens well might spare);
But she with such a zeal the cause embraced
(As women, where they will, are all in haste),

The father, mother, and the kin beside,
Were overborne by fury of the tide ;
With full consent of all she changed her state ;
Resistless in her love, as in her hate.

By her example warned, the rest beware ;
More easy, less imperious, were the fair ;
And that one hunting, which the devil designed
For one fair female, lost him half the kind.

Cymon and Iphigenia.

FROM BOCCACE.

—·—

OLD as I am, for lady's love unfit,
The power of beauty I remember yet,
Which once inflamed my soul, and still inspires my
If love be folly, the severe divine   [wit.
Has felt that folly, though he censures mine ;
Pollutes the pleasures of a chaste embrace,
Acts what I write, and propagates in grace,
With riotous excess, a priestly race.
Suppose him free, and that I forge the offence,
He showed the way, perverting first my sense :
In malice witty, and with venom fraught,
He makes me speak the things I never thought.
Compute the gains of his ungoverned zeal ;
Ill suits his cloth the praise of railing well.
The world will think that what we loosely write,
Though now arraigned, he read with some delight ;
Because he seems to chew the cud again,
When his broad comment makes the text too plain,
And teaches more in one explaining page
Than all the double meanings of the stage.
    What needs he paraphrase on what we mean ?
We were at first but wanton ; he's obscene.
I nor my fellows nor myself excuse ;
But love's the subject of the comic muse ;
Nor can we write without it, nor would you
A tale of only dry instruction view.
Nor love is always of a vicious kind,
But oft to virtuous acts inflames the mind,

Awakes the sleepy vigour of the soul,
And, brushing o'er, adds motion to the pool.
Love, studious how to please, improves our parts
With polished manners, and adorns with arts.
Love first invented verse, and formed the rhyme,
The motion measured, harmonised the chime ;
To liberal acts enlarged the narrow-souled,
Softened the fierce, and made the coward bold ;
The world, when waste, he peopled with increase,
And warring nations reconciled in peace.
Ormond, the first, and all the fair may find,
In this one legend to their fame designed,   [mind.
When beauty fires the blood, how love exalts the

    In that sweet isle, where Venus keeps her court,
And every grace, and all the loves, resort ;
Where either sex is formed of softer earth,
And takes the bent of pleasure from their birth ;
There lived a Cyprian lord, above the rest
Wise, wealthy, with a numerous issue blest.
    But, as no gift of fortune is sincere,
Was only wanting in a worthy heir :
His eldest born, a goodly youth to view,
Excelled the rest in shape and outward show,
Fair, tall, his limbs with due proportion joined,
But of a heavy, dull, degenerate mind.
His soul belied the features of his face ;
Beauty was there, but beauty in disgrace.
A clownish mien, a voice with rustic sound,
And stupid eyes that ever loved the ground,
He looked like nature's error, as the mind
And body were not of a piece designed,
But made for two, and by mistake in one were joined.
    The ruling rod, the father's forming care,
Were exercised in vain on wit's despair ;
The more informed, the less he understood,
And deeper sunk by floundering in the mud.
Now scorned of all, and grown the public shame,
The people from Galesus changed his name,
And Cymon called, which signifies a brute ;
So well his name did with his nature suit.

His father, when he found his labour lost,
And care employed that answered not the cost,
Chose an ungrateful object to remove,
And loathed to see what nature made him love ;
So to his country farm the fool confined ;
Rude work well suited with a rustic mind.
Thus to the wilds the sturdy Cymon went,
A squire among the swains, and pleased with ban-
    ishment.
His corn and cattle were his only care,
And his supreme delight a country fair.

  It happened on a summer's holiday,
That to the greenwood shade he took his way ;
For Cymon shunned the church, and used not
    much to pray.
His quarter-staff, which he could ne'er forsake,
Hung half before and half behind his back.
He trudged along, unknowing what he sought,
And whistled as he went, for want of thought.

  By chance conducted, or by thirst constrained,
The deep recesses of the grove he gained ;
Where, in a plain defended by the wood,
Crept through the matted grass a crystal flood,
By which an alabaster fountain stood ;
And on the margin of the fount was laid,
Attended by her slaves, a sleeping maid ;
Like Dian and her nymphs, when, tired with sport
To rest by cool Eurotas they resort.
The dame herself the goddess well expressed,
Not more distinguished by her purple vest
Than by the charming features of her face,
And, even in slumber, a superior grace :
Her comely limbs composed with decent care,
Her body shaded with a slight cymarr ;
Her bosom to the view was only bare :
Where two beginning paps were scarcely spied,
For yet their places were but signified :
The fanning wind upon her bosom blows,
To meet the fanning wind the bosom rose ;
The fanning wind and purling streams continue her
    repose.

The fool of nature stood with stupid eyes,
And gaping mouth that testified surprise,
Fixed on her face, nor could remove his sight,
New as he was to love, and novice in delight :
Long mute he stood, and leaning on his staff,
His wonder witnessed with an idiot laugh ;
Then would have spoke, but by his glimmering sense
First found his want of words, and feared offence :
Doubted for what he was he should be known,
By his clown-accent and his country-tone.
Through the rude chaos thus the running light
Shot the first ray that pierced the native night :
Then day and darkness in the mass were mixed,
Till gathered in a globe the beams were fixed :
Last shone the sun, who, radiant in his sphere,
Illumined heaven and earth, and rolled around the
So reason in this brutal soul began :   [year.
Love made him first suspect he was a man ;
Love made him doubt his broad barbarian sound ;
By love his want of words and wit he found ;
That sense of want prepared the future way
To knowledge, and disclosed the promise of a day.
What not his father's care nor tutor's art
Could plant with pains in his unpolished heart,
The best instructor, Love, at once inspired,
As barren grounds to fruitfulness are fired ;
Love taught him shame, and shame with love at
      strife
Soon taught the sweet civilities of life.
His gross material soul at once could find
Somewhat in her excelling all her kind ;
Exciting a desire till then unknown,
Somewhat unfound or found in her alone.
This made the first impression on his mind,
Above, but just above, the brutal kind.
For beasts can like, but not distinguish too,
Nor their own liking by reflection know ;
Nor why they like or this or t'other face,
Or judge of this or that peculiar grace ;
But love in gross, and stupidly admire ;
As flies, allured by light, approach the fire.

Thus our man-beast, approaching by degrees,
First likes the whole, then separates what he sees :
On several parts a several praise bestows,
The ruby lips, the well-proportioned nose,
The snowy skin, the raven glossy hair,
The dimpled cheek, the forehead rising fair,
And even in sleep itself a smiling air.
From thence his eyes descending viewed the rest,
Her plump round arms, white hands, and heaving
    breast.
Long on the last he dwelt, though every part
A pointed arrow sped to pierce his heart.
    Thus in a trice a judge of beauty grown
(A judge erected from a country clown),
He longed to see her eyes in slumber hid,
And wished his own could pierce within the lid.
He would have waked her, but restrained his thought,
And love new-born the first good manners taught.
An awful fear his ardent wish withstood,
Nor durst disturb the goddess of the wood ;
For such she seemed by her celestial face,
Excelling all the rest of human race ;
And things divine, by common sense he knew,
Must be devoutly seen at distant view :
So checking his desire, with trembling heart
Gazing he stood, nor would nor could depart ;
Fixed as a pilgrim wildered in his way,
Who dares not stir by night, for fear to stray ;
But stands with awful eyes to watch the dawn of day.
    At length awaking, Iphigene the fair
(So was the beauty called who caused his care)
Unclosed her eyes, and double day revealed,
While those of all her slaves in sleep were sealed.
    The slavering cudden, propped upon his staff,
Stood ready gaping with a grinning laugh,
To welcome her awake, nor durst begin
To speak, but wisely kept the fool within.
Then she: " What make you, Cymon, here alone ?"
(For Cymon's name was round the country known,
Because descended of a noble race,
And for a soul ill sorted with his face.)

But still the sot stood silent with surprise,
With fixed regard on her new-opened eyes,
And in his breast received the envenomed dart,
A tickling pain that pleased amid the smart,
But conscious of her form, with quick distrust
She saw his sparkling eyes, and feared his brutal lust.
This to prevent, she waked her sleepy crew,
And rising hasty took a short adieu.
Then Cymon first his rustic voice essayed,
With proffered service to the parting maid
To see her safe; his hand she long denied,
But took at length, ashamed of such a guide.
So Cymon led her home, and leaving there,
No more would to his country clowns repair,
But sought his father's house, with better mind,
Refusing in the farm to be confined.
The father wondered at the son's return,
And knew not whether to rejoice or mourn;
But doubtfully received, expecting still
To learn the secret causes of his altered will.
Nor was he long delayed: the first request
He made, was like his brothers to be dressed,
And, as his birth required, above the rest.
With ease his suit was granted by his sire,
Distinguishing his heir by rich attire:
His body thus adorned, he next designed
With liberal arts to cultivate his mind;
He sought a tutor of his own accord,
And studied lessons he before abhorred.
Thus the man-child advanced, and learned so fast,
That in short time his equals he surpassed:
His brutal manners from his breast exiled,
His mien he fashioned, and his tongue he filed;
In every exercise of all admired,
He seemed, nor only seemed, but was inspired:
Inspired by love, whose business is to please;
He rode, he fenced, he moved with graceful ease,
More famed for sense, for courtly carriage more,
Than for his brutal folly known before.
What then of altered Cymon shall we say,
But that the fire which choked in ashes lay,

A load too heavy for his soul to move,
Was upward blown below, and brushed away by
   love?
Love made an active progress through his mind.
The dusky parts he cleared, the gross refined,
The drowsy waked; and, as he went, impressed
The Maker's image on the human breast.
Thus was the man amended by desire,
And, though he loved perhaps with too much fire,
His father all his faults with reason scanned,
And liked an error of the better hand;
Excused the excess of passion in his mind,
By flames too fierce, perhaps too much refined:
So Cymon, since his sire indulged his will,
Impetuous loved, and would be Cymon still;
Galesus he disowned, and chose to bear   [fair.
The name of fool, confirmed and bishoped by the
   To Cipseus by his friends his suit he moved,
Cipseus the father of the fair he loved;
But he was pre-engaged by former ties,
While Cymon was endeavouring to be wise;
And Iphigene, obliged by former vows,
Had given her faith to wed a foreign spouse:
Her sire and she to Rhodian Pasimond,
Though both repenting, were by promise bound,
Nor could retract; and thus, as fate decreed,
Though better loved, he spoke too late to speed.
   The doom was past; the ship already sent
Did all his tardy diligence prevent;
Sighed to herself the fair unhappy maid,
While stormy Cymon thus in secret said:
" The time is come for Iphigene to find
The miracle she wrought upon my mind;
Her charms have made me man, her ravished love
In rank shall place me with the blessed above.
For mine by love, by force she shall be mine,
Or death, if force should fail, shall finish my design."
   Resolved he said; and rigged with speedy care
A vessel strong, and well equipped for war.
The secret ship with chosen friends he stored,
And bent to die, or conquer, went aboard.

Ambushed he lay behind the Cyprian shore,
Waiting the sail that all his wishes bore;
Nor long expected, for the following tide
Sent out the hostile ship and beauteous bride.
    To Rhodes the rival bark directly steered,
When Cymon sudden at her back appeared,
And stopped her flight: then standing on his prow,
In haughty terms he thus defied the foe:
"Or strike your sails at summons, or prepare
To prove the last extremities of war."
Thus warned, the Rhodians for the fight provide;
Already were the vessels side by side,
These obstinate to save, and those to seize the bride.
But Cymon soon his crooked grapples cast,
Which with tenacious hold his foes embraced,'
And, armed with sword and shield, amid the press
        he passed.
Fierce was the fight, but hastening to his prey,
By force the furious lover freed his way;
Himself alone dispersed the Rhodian crew,
The weak disdained, the valiant overthrew;
Cheap conquest for his following friends remained,
He reaped the field, and they but only gleaned.
    His victory confessed, the foes retreat,
And cast their weapons at the victor's feet.
Whom thus he cheered: "O Rhodian youth, I fought
For love alone, nor other booty sought;
Your lives are safe; your vessel I resign,
Yours be your own, restoring what is mine;
In Iphigene I claim my rightful due,
Robbed by my rival, and detained by you:
Your Pasimond a lawless bargain drove,
The parent could not sell the daughter's love;
Or if he could, my love disdains the laws,
And like a king by conquest gains his cause;
Where arms take place, all other pleas are vain;
Love taught me force, and force shall love maintain.
You, what by strength you could not keep, release,
And at an easy ransom buy your peace."
    Fear on the conquered side soon signed the
And Iphigene to Cymon was restored.   [accord,

While to his arms the blushing bride he took,
To seeming sadness she composed her look ;
As if by force subjected to his will,
Though pleased, dissembling, and a woman still.
And, for she wept, he wiped her falling tears,
And prayed her to dismiss her empty fears ; .
" For yours I am," he said, "and have deserved
Your love much better, whom so long I served,
Than he to whom your formal father tied
Your vows, and sold a slave, not sent a bride."
Thus while he spoke, he seized the willing prey,
As Paris bore the Spartan spouse away.
Faintly she screamed, and even her eyes confessed
She rather would be thought, than was, distressed.
  Who now exults but Cymon in his mind ?
Vain hopes and empty joys of human kind,
Proud of the present, to the future blind !
Secure of fate, while Cymon ploughs the sea,
And steers to Candy with his conquered prey,
Scarce the third glass of measured hours was run,
When like a fiery meteor sunk the sun,
The promise of a storm ; the shifting gales
Forsake by fits and fill the flagging sails ;
Hoarse murmurs of the main from far were heard;
And night came on, not by degrees prepared,
But all at once ; at once the winds arise,
The thunders roll, the forky lightning flies.
In vain the master issues out commands,
In vain the trembling sailors ply their hands ;
The tempest unforeseen prevents their care,
And from the first they labour in despair.
The giddy ship betwixt the winds and tides,
Forced back and forwards, in a circle rides,
Stunned with the different blows; then shoots amain,
Till counterbuffed she stops, and sleeps again.
Not more aghast the proud archangel fell,
Plunged from the height of heaven to deepest hell,
Than stood the lover of his love possessed,
Now cursed the more, the more he had been blessed
More anxious for her danger than his own,
Death he defies, but would be lost alone.

Sad Iphigene to womanish complaints
Adds pious prayers, and wearies all the saints;
Even if she could, her love she would repent,
But since she cannot, dreads the punishment:
Her forfeit faith and Pasimond betrayed
Are ever present, and her crime upbraid.
She blames herself, nor blames her lover less;
Augments her anger as her fears increase;
From her own back the burden would remove,
And lays the load on his ungoverned love,
Which interposing durst, in Heaven's despite,
Invade and violate another's right:
The powers incensed a while deferred his pain,
And made him master of his vows in vain:
But soon they punished his presumptuous pride;
That for his daring enterprise she died,
Who rather not resisted than complied.
    Then, impotent of mind, with altered sense,
She hugged the offender, and forgave the offence,
Sex to the last.   Meantime with sails declined
The wandering vessel drove before the wind,
Tossed and retossed, aloft, and then alow;
Nor port they seek, nor certain course they know,
But every moment wait the coming blow.
Thus blindly driven, by breaking day they viewed
The land before them, and their fears renewed;
The land was welcome, but the tempest bore
The threatened ship against a rocky shore.
A winding bay was near; to this they bent,
And just escaped; their force already spent.
Secure from storms, and panting from the sea,
The land unknown at leisure they survey;
And saw (but soon their sickly sight withdrew)
The rising towers of Rhodes at distant view;
And cursed the hostile shore of Pasimond,
Saved from the seas, and shipwrecked on the
    ground.
The frighted sailors tried their strength in vain
To turn the stern, and tempt the stormy main;
But the stiff wind withstood the labouring oar,
And forced them forward on the fatal shore!

The crooked keel now bites the Rhodian strand,
And the ship moored constrains the crew to land :
Yet still they might be safe, because unknown ;
But as ill fortune seldom comes alone,
The vessel they dismissed was driven before,
Already sheltered on their native shore ;
Known each, they know, but each with change of
 cheer ;
The vanquished side exults ; the victors fear
Not them but theirs, made prisoners ere they fight,
Despairing conquest, and deprived of flight.
 The country rings around with loud alarms,
And raw in fields the rude militia swarms ;
Mouths without hands ; maintained at vast expense,
In peace a charge, in war a weak defence ;
Stout once a month they march, a blustering band,
And ever, but in times of need, at hand ;
This was the morn when, issuing on the guard,
Drawn up in rank and file they stood prepared
Of seeming arms to make a short essay,
Then hasten to be drunk, the business of the day.
 The cowards would have fled, but that they knew
Themselves so many and their foes so few ;
But crowding on, the last the first impel,
Till overborne with weight the Cyprians fell.
Cymon enslaved, who first the war begun,
And Iphigene once more is lost and won.
 Deep in a dungeon was the captive cast,
Deprived of day, and held in fetters fast ;
His life was only spared at their request,
Whom taken he so nobly had released :
But Iphigenia was the ladies' care,
Each in their turn addressed to treat the fair ;
While Pasimond and his the nuptial feast prepare.
 Her secret soul to Cymon was inclined,
But she must suffer what her fates assigned ;
So passive is the church of womankind.
What worse to Cymon could his fortune deal,
Rolled to the lowest spoke of all her wheel ?
It rested to dismiss the downward weight,
Or raise him upward to his former height ;

The latter pleased; and love (concerned the most)
Prepared the amends for what by love he lost.
  The sire of Pasimond had left a son,
Though younger, yet for courage early known,
Ormisda called, to whom, by promise tied,
A Rhodian beauty was the destined bride;
Cassandra was her name, above the rest
Renowned for birth, with fortune amply blessed.
Lysimachus, who ruled the Rhodian state,
Was then by choice their annual magistrate;
He loved Cassandra too with equal fire,
But fortune had not favoured his desire;
Crossed by her friends, by her not disapproved,
Nor yet preferred, or like Ormisda loved:
So stood the affair: some little hope remained,
That, should his rival chance to lose, he gained.
  Meantime young Pasimond his marriage pressed,
Ordained the nuptial day, prepared the feast;
And frugally resolved (the charge to shun,
Which would be double should he wed alone),
To join his brother's bridal with his own.
  Lysimachus, oppressed with mortal grief,
Received the news, and studied quick relief:
The fatal day approached; if force were used,
The magistrate his public trust abused,
To justice liable, as law required,
For when his office ceased, his power expired:
While power remained, the means were in his
    hand
By force to seize, and then forsake the land:
Betwixt extremes he knew not how to move,
A slave to fame, but more a slave to love:
Restraining others, yet himself not free,
Made impotent by power, debased by dignity.
Both sides he weighed: but after much debate,
The man prevailed above the magistrate.
  Love never fails to master what he finds,
But works a different way in different minds,
The fool enlightens, and the wise he blinds.
This youth proposing to possess and scape,
Began in murder, to conclude in rape:

Unpraised by me, though Heaven sometime may
    bless
An impious act with undeserved success :
The great, it seems, are privileged alone
To punish all injustice but their own.
But here I stop, not daring to proceed,
Yet blush to flatter an unrighteous deed ;
For crimes are but permitted, not decreed.

    Resolved on force, his wit the prætor bent
To find the means that might secure the event ;
Nor long he laboured, for his lucky thought
In captive Cymon found the friend he sought.
The example pleased : the cause and crime the same,
An injured lover and a ravished dame.
How much he durst he knew by what he dared,
The less he had to lose, the less he cared
To menage loathsome life when love was the reward.

    This pondered well, and fixed on his intent,
In depth of night he for the prisoner sent ;
In secret sent, the public view to shun,
Then with a sober smile he thus begun :
" The Powers above, who bounteously bestow
Their gifts and graces on mankind below,
Yet prove our merit first, nor blindly give
To such as are not worthy to receive :
For valour and for virtue they provide
Their due reward, but first they must be tried :
These fruitful seeds within your mind they sowed ;
'Twas yours to improve the talent they bestowed ;
They gave you to be born of noble kind,
They gave you love to lighten up your mind
And purge the grosser parts ; they gave you care
To please, and courage to deserve the fair.

    Thus far they tried you, and by proof they found
The grain entrusted in a grateful ground :
But still the great experiment remained,
They suffered you to lose the prize you gained,
That you might learn the gift was theirs alone,
And, when restored, to them the blessing own.
Restored it soon will be ; the means prepared
The difficulty smoothed, the danger shared :

But be yourself, the care to me resign,
Then Iphigene is yours, Cassandra mine.
Your rival Pasimond pursues your life,
Impatient to revenge his ravished wife,
But not yet his; to-morrow is behind,
And love our fortunes in one band has joined :
Two brothers are our foes, Ormisda mine
As much declared as Pasimond is thine :
To-morrow must their common vows be tied :
With Love to friend, and Fortune for our guide,
Let both resolve to die, or each redeem a bride.
  Right I have none, nor hast thou much to plead;
'Tis force, when done, must justify the deed :
Our task performed, we next prepare for flight :
And let the losers talk in vain of right :
We with the fair will sail before the wind ;
If they are grieved, I leave the laws behind.
Speak thy resolves : if now thy courage droop,
Despair in prison and abandon hope ;
But if thou darest in arms thy love regain
(For liberty without thy love were vain),
Then second my design to seize the prey,   [way."
Or lead to second rape, for well thou knowest the
  Said Cymon, overjoyed : "Do thou propose
The means to fight, and only show the foes :
For from the first, when love had fired my mind,
Resolved, I left the care of life behind."
  To this the bold Lysimachus replied,
"Let Heaven be neuter and the sword decide :
The spousals are prepared, already play
The minstrels, and provoke the tardy day :
By this the brides are waked, their grooms are
    dressed ;
All Rhodes is summoned to the nuptial feast,
All but myself, the sole unbidden guest.
Unbidden though I am, I will be there,
And, joined by thee, intend to join the fair.
  "Now hear the rest ; when day resigns the light,
And cheerful torches gild the jolly night,
Be ready at my call ; my chosen few
With arms administered shall aid thy crew.

Then entering unexpected will we seize
Our destined prey, from men dissolved in ease,
By wine disabled, unprepared for fight,
And hastening to the seas, suborn our flight:
The seas are ours, for I command the fort,
A ship well manned expects us in the port:
If they, or if their friends, the prize contest,
Death shall attend the man who dares resist."
  It pleased; the prisoner to his hold retired,
His troop with equal emulation fired,
All fixed to fight, and all their wonted work required.
  The sun arose; the streets were thronged around,
The palace opened, and the posts were crowned.
The double bridegroom at the door attends
The expected spouse, and entertains the friends:
They meet, they lead to church, the priests invoke
The Powers, and feed the flames with fragrant smoke.
This done, they feast, and at the close of night
By kindled torches vary their delight,
These lead the lively dance, and those the brimming
      bowls invite.
  Now, at the appointed place and hour assigned,
With souls resolved the ravishers were joined:
Three bands are formed; the first is sent before
To favour the retreat and guard the shore;
The second at the palace gate is placed,
And up the lofty stairs ascend the last:
A peaceful troop they seem with shining vests,
But coats of mail beneath secure their breasts.
  Dauntless they enter, Cymon at their head,
And find the feast renewed, the table spread:
Sweet voices, mixed with instrumental sounds,
Ascend the vaulted roof, the vaulted roof rebounds.
When, like the harpies, rushing through the hall
The sudden troop appears, the tables fall,
Their smoking load is on the pavement thrown;
Each ravisher prepares to seize his own:
The brides, invaded with a rude embrace,
Shriek out for aid, confusion fills the place.
Quick to redeem the prey their plighted lords
Advance, the palace gleams with shining swords.

But late is all defence, and succour vain ;
The rape is made, the ravishers remain :
Two sturdy slaves were only sent before
To bear the purchased prize in safety to the shore.
The troop retires, the lovers close the rear,
With forward faces not confessing fear :
Backward they move, but scorn their pace to mend ;
Then seek the stairs, and with slow haste descend.
    Fierce Pasimond, their passage to prevent,
Thrust full on Cymon's back in his descent,
The blade returned unbathed, and to the handle
    bent.
Stout Cymon soon remounts, and cleft in two
His rival's head with one descending blow :
And as the next in rank Ormisda stood,
He turned the point ; the sword inured to blood
Bored his unguarded breast, which poured a purple
    flood.
    With vowed revenge the gathering crowd pursues,
The ravishers turn head, the fight renews ;
The hall is heaped with corps ; the sprinkled gore
Besmears the walls, and floats the marble floor.
Dispersed at length, the drunken squadron flies,
The victors to their vessel bear the prize,
And hear behind loud groans, and lamentable cries.
    The crew with merry shouts their anchors weigh,
Then ply their oars, and brush the buxom sea,
While troops of gathered Rhodians crowd the
    quay.
What should the people do when left alone ?
The governor and government are gone ;
The public wealth to foreign parts conveyed ;
Some troops disbanded, and the rest unpaid.
Rhodes is the sovereign of the sea no more ;
Their ships unrigged, and spent their naval store ;
They neither could defend nor can pursue,
But grind their teeth, and cast a helpless view :
In vain with darts a distant war they try,
Short, and more short, the missive weapons fly.
Meanwhile the ravishers their crimes enjoy,
And flying sails and sweeping oars employ :

The cliffs of Rhodes in little space are lost ;
Jove's isle they seek, nor Jove denies his coast.
   In safety landed on the Candian shore,
With generous wines their spirits they restore ;
There Cymon with his Rhodian friend resides,
Both court and wed at once the willing brides.
A war ensues, the Cretans own their cause,
Stiff to defend their hospitable laws :
Both parties lose by turns, and neither wins,
Till peace, propounded by a truce, begins.
The kindred of the slain forgive the deed,
But a short exile must for show precede :
The term expired, from Candia they remove,
And happy each at home enjoys his love,

A Song for St. Cecilia's Day.

November 22, 1687.

—❧❧—

1.

FROM harmony, from heavenly harmony
    This universal frame began ;
   When Nature underneath a heap
    Of jarring atoms lay,
   And could not heave her head,
The tuneful voice was heard from high,
    Arise, ye more than dead.
Then cold and hot and moist and dry
   In order to their stations leap,
    And music's power obey.
From harmony, from heavenly harmony
    This universal frame began :
    From harmony to harmony
Through all the compass of the notes it ran,
The diapason closing full in Man.

2.

What passion cannot music raise and quell?
    When Jubal struck the chorded shell,
   His listening brethren stood around,
    And, wondering, on their faces fell
   To worship that celestial sound :
Less than a god they thought there could not
    dwell
    Within the hollow of that shell,
    That spoke so sweetly and so well :
What passion cannot music raise and quell?

3.

The trumpet's loud clangour
   Excites us to arms
With shrill notes of anger
   And mortal alarms.
The double double double beat
   Of the thundering drum
   Cries, "Hark! the foes come :
Charge, charge, 'tis too late to retreat."

4.

The soft complaining flute
In dying notes discovers
The woes of hopeless lovers,
Whose dirge is whispered by the warbling lute.

5.

Sharp violins proclaim
Their jealous pangs and desperation,
Fury, frantic indignation,
Depth of pains and height of passion,
   For the fair, disdainful dame.

6.

But oh! what art can teach,
What human voice can reach
   The sacred organ's praise?
Notes inspiring holy love,
Notes that wing their heavenly ways
   To mend the choirs above.

7.

Orpheus could lead the savage race,
And trees unrooted left their place,
   Sequacious of the lyre ;
But bright Cecilia raised the wonder higher :
When to her organ vocal breath was given,
An angel heard, and straight appeared,
   Mistaking earth for heaven.

GRAND CHORUS.

As from the power of sacred lays
   The spheres began to move,
And sung the great Creator's praise
   To all the blessed above;
So when the last and dreadful hour
This crumbling pageant shall devour,
The trumpet shall be heard on high,
The dead shall live, the living die,
And music shall untune the sky.

Alexander's Feast;

OR, THE POWER OF MUSIC.

A SONG IN HONOUR OF ST. CECILIA'S DAY: 1697.

—❧—

I.

'TWAS at the royal feast for Persia won
    By Philip's warlike son :
    Aloft in awful state
    The godlike hero sate
    On his imperial throne ;
  His valiant peers were placed around ;
Their brows with roses and with myrtles
    bound
  (So should desert in arms be crowned).
The lovely Thais, by his side,
Sate like a blooming Eastern bride,
In flower of youth and beauty's pride.
    Happy, happy, happy pair !
      None but the brave,
      None but the brave,
None but the brave deserves the fair.

CHORUS.

  Happy, happy, happy pair !
    None but the brave,
    None but the brave,
None but the brave deserves the fair.

2.

Timotheus, placed on high
Amid the tuneful choir,
With flying fingers touched the lyre :
The trembling notes ascend the sky,
And heavenly joys inspire.
The song began from Jove,
Who left his blissful seats above
(Such is the power of mighty love).
A dragon's fiery form belied the god :
Sublime on radiant spires he rode,
When he to fair Olympia pressed :
And while he sought her snowy breast,
Then round her slender waist he curled,
And stamped an image of himself, a sovereign of
the world.
The listening crowd admire the lofty sound,
" A present deity ! " they shout around ;
" A present deity ! " the vaulted roofs rebound
With ravished ears
The monarch hears,
Assumes the god
Affects to nod,
And seems to shake the spheres.

CHORUS.

With ravished ears
The monarch hears,
Assumes the god,
Affects to nod,
And seems to shake the spheres.

3.

The praise of Bacchus then the sweet musician sung,
Of Bacchus ever fair, and ever young.
The jolly god in triumph comes ;
Sound the trumpets, beat the drums ;
Flushed with a purple grace
He shows his honest face :
Now give the hautboys breath ; he comes, he comes.

Bacchus, ever fair and young,
  Drinking joys did first ordain;
Bacchus' blessings are a treasure,
Drinking is the soldier's pleasure;
    Rich the treasure,
    Sweet the pleasure,
  Sweet is pleasure after pain.

CHORUS.

Bacchus' blessings are a treasure,
Drinking is the soldier's pleasure;
    Rich the treasure,
    Sweet the pleasure,
  Sweet is pleasure after pain.

4.

Soothed with the sound, the king grew vain;
  Fought all his battles o'er again;
And thrice he routed all his foes, and thrice he slew
    the slain.
  The master saw the madness rise,
  His glowing cheeks, his ardent eyes;
And while he heaven and earth defied,
Changed his hand, and checked his pride.
    He chose a mournful muse,
    Soft pity to infuse;
  He sung Darius great and good,
    By too severe a fate
Fallen, fallen, fallen, fallen,
  Fallen from his high estate,
And weltering in his blood;
Deserted at his utmost need
By those his former bounty fed;
On the bare earth exposed he lies,
With not a friend to close his eyes.
With downcast looks the joyless victor sate,
    Revolving in his altered soul
      The various turns of chance below;
    And, now and then, a sigh he stole,
      And tears began to flow.

CHORUS.

Revolving in his altered soul
The various turns of chance below;
And, now and then, a sigh he stole,
And tears began to flow.

5.

The mighty master smiled to see
That love was in the next degree;
'Twas but a kindred sound to move,
For pity melts the mind to love.
Softly sweet, in Lydian measures,
Soon he soothed his soul to pleasures.
"War," he sung, "is toil and trouble;
Honour but an empty bubble;
Never ending, still beginning,
Fighting still, and still destroying:
If the world be worth thy winning,
Think, O think it worth enjoying:
Lovely Thais sits beside thee,
Take the good the gods provide thee."
The many rend the skies with loud applause;
So Love was crowned, but Music won the cause.
The prince, unable to conceal his pain,
Gazed on the fair
Who caused his care,
And sighed and looked, sighed and looked,
Sighed and looked, and sighed again;
At length, with love and wine at once oppressed,
The vanquished victor sunk upon her breast.

CHORUS.

The prince, unable to conceal his pain,
Gazed on the fair
Who caused his care,
And sighed and looked, sighed and looked,
Sighed and looked, and sighed again;
At length, with love and wine at once oppressed,
The vanquished victor sunk upon her breast.

6.

Now strike the golden lyre again ;
A louder yet, and yet a louder strain.
Break his bands of sleep asunder,
And rouse him, like a rattling peal of thunder.
    Hark, hark, the horrid sound
      Has raised up his head ;
      As awaked from the dead,
    And amazed, he stares around.
  " Revenge, revenge ! " Timotheus cries,
    " See the Furies arise ;
    See the snakes that they rear,
    How they hiss in their hair,
And the sparkles that flash from their eyes !
    Behold a ghastly band,
    Each a torch in his hand !
Those are Grecian ghosts, that in battle were
    slain
      And unburied remain
      Inglorious on the plain :
      Give the vengeance due
      To the valiant crew.
Behold how they toss their torches on high,
  How they point to the Persian abodes,
And glittering temples of their hostile gods."
The princes applaud with a furious joy ;
And the king seized a flambeau with zeal to
    destroy ;
    Thais led the way,
    To light him to his prey,
And, like another Helen, fired another Troy.

CHORUS.

And the king seized a flambeau with zeal to
    destroy ;
    Thais led the way,
    To light him to his prey,
And, like another Helen, fired another Troy.

7.

Thus long ago,
Ere heaving bellows learned to blow,
While organs yet were mute,
Timotheus, to his breathing flute
And sounding lyre,
Could swell the soul to rage, or kindle soft desire.
At last divine Cecilia came,
Inventress of the vocal frame;
The sweet enthusiast, from ber sacred store,
Enlarged the former narrow bounds,
And added length to solemn sounds,
With nature's mother-wit, and arts unknown before.
Let old Timotheus yield the prize,
Or both divide the crown:
He raised a mortal to the skies;
She drew an angel down.

GRAND CHORUS.

At last divine Cecilia came,
Inventress of the vocal frame;
The sweet enthusiast, from her sacred store,
Enlarged the former narrow bounds,
And added length to solemn sounds,
With nature's mother-wit, and arts unknown before.
Let old Timotheus yield the prize,
Or both divide the crown:
He raised a mortal to the skies;
She drew an angel down.

Printed by BALLANTYNE, HANSON & CO.
Edinburgh and London.